PRAISE FOR *WHAT I KNOW ABOUT YOU*

Winner of the French Booksellers' Prize 2024
Winner of the Prix Femina des Lycéens 2023
Winner of the Prix des Cinq Continents de la Francophonie 2024
Winner of the Bourse de la Découverte Fondation Pierre de
    Monaco 2023
Winner of the Prix Première Plume 2023
Winner of the Prix des Libraires en Seine 2024
Winner of the Prix du Club des Irrésistibles 2024
Winner of the Prix Littéraire Evok 2024
Winner of the Prix du Conseil des Arts et des Lettres du
    Québec 2024
Shortlisted for the Prix Femina 2023
Shortlisted for the Prix Renaudot 2023
Shortlisted for the Prix du Roman Fnac 2023
Shortlisted for the Quebec Booksellers' Prize 2024

'The most awarded novel of the year.' – *Le Point*

'Magic … intimate and majestic.'
        – Jean-Baptiste Andrea, winner of the Prix Goncourt 2023

'A debut that reads like a classic.' – *Le Figaro*

'Impressive … A masterful, thrilling debut.' – *L'Express*

'One of the best novels of recent years.' – *Fugues*

'Razor-sharp yet sensual prose … plumbs the depths of a man torn
between two worlds and two eras, for a vibrant portrait of a changing
society … Dazzling.' – *Le Devoir*

T0286508

'A delicate, sensual, political debut.' – *Libération*

'A sublime story of absence and reconciliation.' – *Le Parisien*

'Certain novels leave an indelible mark – this is one of them.'
                                                    – *Les Libraires*

'A writer who charts his own course, polishing each sentence until it conveys the totality of the observable world, from the smallest gesture and look to the displacements contained in our life choices. A story of love, memory, and devastation.'
                    – Jury statement, Prix des Cinq Continents 2024

'An intimate conversation fraught with things left unsaid and secrets revealed, told with a delicate understatement. Masterful.'
                    – Shirley Saver, jury chair, Prix Première Plume 2023

'So powerfully resonant and ingeniously constructed, it is hard to believe this is a first novel.' – *Le Soleil*

'The writing is silken, suggestive, skilful, and touching.' – *La Presse*

WHAT
I KNOW
ABOUT
YOU

ÉRIC CHACOUR

translated by
PABLO STRAUSS

COACH HOUSE BOOKS, TORONTO

Originally published in French by Les Éditions Alto as *Ce que je sais de toi* by
   Éric Chacour
Copyright © Éric Chacour and Éditions Alto, 2023
English translation © Pablo Strauss, 2024

First English-language edition

Published with the generous assistance of the Canada Council for the Arts and
the Ontario Arts Council. Coach House Books also acknowledges the support of
the Government of Canada through the Canada Book Fund.

LIBRARY AND ARCHIVES CANADA CATALOGUING IN PUBLICATION

Title: What I know about you / by Éric Chacour ; translated by Pablo Strauss.
Other titles: Ce que je sais de toi. English
Names: Chacour, Éric, 1983- author. | Strauss, Pablo, translator
Description: Translation of: Ce que je sais de toi.
Identifiers: Canadiana (print) 2024041781X | Canadiana (ebook) 20240417828
| ISBN 9781552454855 (softcover) | ISBN 9781770568150 (EPUB) | ISBN
9781770568167 (PDF)
Subjects: LCGFT: Novels.
Classification: LCC PS8605.H32339 C413 2024 | DDC C843/.6—dc23

What I Know About You is available as an ebook: ISBN 978 1 77056 815 0 (EPUB),
ISBN 978 1 77056 816 7 (PDF)

Purchase of the print version of this book entitles you to a free digital copy. To
claim your ebook of this title, please email sales@chbooks.com with proof of
purchase. (Coach House Books reserves the right to terminate the free digital
download offer at any time.)

For the ones who taught me to love Egypt.
For the women.

YOU

1

Cairo, 1961

'What kind of car do you want when you grow up?'

He'd simply asked a question, but you hadn't yet learned to be wary of simple questions. You were twelve, your sister ten, walking with your father along the bank of the Nile through Zamalek's residential section. Swept along by the boisterous procession of traffic, your gaze wandered to the lotus-shaped spire of the Cairo Tower that had recently sprung up. *The tallest in all of Africa,* people said with pride. *And built by a Melkite, too!*

Your sister, Nesrine, hadn't waited for your answer.

'That one, Baba. The big red one over there.'

'What about you, Tarek?'

It wasn't something you had ever thought about.

'How about … a donkey?' You felt a need to justify yourself. 'Not so loud.'

Your father's forced laugh made it clear that your answer was beneath consideration. Or was he trying to convince himself that you were only kidding? Nesrine teased loose a lock of her dark hair and curled it around her index finger, a habit of hers when at a loss for words. Clearly convinced that if she pestered him enough she would find herself behind the wheel of a convertible that very afternoon, she said it again, ratcheting up the enthusiasm.

'The red one, Baba! With the roof that opens!'

Your father looked at you, still waiting for your answer. Just to make him happy, you chose one at random.

'I'd take that black one, over there. The one stopped at the corner.'

First your father cleared his throat, then he proceeded to explain.

'Good choice. A fine American car: a Cadillac. You know they're expensive, right? You'll need a good job. Engineer or doctor?'

He was talking to you without looking at you, focused on the pipe he had just placed between his lips. He began by sucking in air through the empty pipe, a routine at once mysterious and habitual. Satisfied with the airflow, he pulled out the pouch of tobacco whose smell was so familiar you couldn't say whether you liked it or not. He filled the bowl, easing his index finger in to arrange the dried leaves, and then painstakingly tamped it down. Each step of this exacting operation was calibrated to yield the right amount of time to think. When he put his pipe back in his mouth to make sure it drew correctly, you knew your time to answer was running out. His clicking lighter rang out like a warning bell. In the smoke of his first puffs, you delivered a half-hearted answer.

'Doctor, I guess … '

He remained still a moment, as if considering a newly tabled offer, then answered gravely.

'Good choice, son. Good choice.'

It was your default choice. You had no idea what engineers did. But that didn't matter. Your father's son would be a doctor, just like him. There was no room for argument. Held between the fingers that would one day teach you your profession, the pipe tamper smothered the embers of your conversation. While your father relit his pipe, you imagined putting on his white lab coat, the one he wore on the ground floor of your villa in Dokki where he saw his patients. You were of an age to have no life plans beyond what others devised for you. Was it really just a matter of age, though?

Your walk proceeded in silence. Each of you seemed absorbed in your thoughts. Once all the tobacco was gone, your father checked his pocket watch. It was inscribed with his initials. Yours, too, as it happened. It was time to go home. The watch always read *time to go home* once all the tobacco had been smoked. Your father's pocket watch and pipe were impeccably synchronized.

That evening you announced it to your mother. You would be a doctor when you grew up, you told her flatly, as you might share some innocuous piece of news. She was as thrilled as if you'd presented her a completed medical degree, first-class honours. Nasser was remaking Egypt into the greatest country in the world, and your mother had decided you would be its leading physician. A little earlier, Nesrine had made you promise you'd buy her a red convertible.

You were twelve. From that day on you would be wary of simple questions.

2

You had no sense when life would begin in earnest. As a child you were a brilliant student. Everyone said your good grades would serve you well later in life. So life would start later, it seemed. Of the succession of moments that made up your life to that point, few traces remain. Lost are the names of those who wore out their backs carrying you around on their shoulders, unnoticed the hours that went into cooking your favourite dish. What you remember are the minor details: how you laughed at Nesrine because she couldn't pronounce the Arabic word for *pyramid*; how you ate frescas on the beach, molasses from the round wafers staining your bathing suits; how you drew pictures with your fingers on the windows that fogged up when Fatheya, your family servant, cooked.

You would stare at the adults, study their body language, inflection, and appearance. From time to time, as if called on to speak by some natural authority, one of them would tell the latest funny story they had heard. Then the listeners' eyes were riveted on the speaker; transformed by this attention, his voice changed, he moved in time with the story, and a palpable tension filled the room. You were enthralled by the effect on the audience, a crowd suddenly breathing as one to the rhythm of the storyteller, who only then began to speak more quickly, gathering momentum in his lead-up to the punchline that all had been waiting for. And as one they would respond with a deep, loud burst of laughter that poured forth spontaneously yet in perfect unison.

The men laughed. But *what* made them laugh? You had no idea. Indecipherable innuendos, impossible exaggerations, unknown words, conspiratorial winks. The mothers' scowls reminding them that there were children present were met with the blithe confidence that they were too young to understand. You, for one, were too young to understand. This language seemed to belong to the adult world, an undiscovered country. Did one simply wash up on those faraway shores one day, scarcely aware of what was happening – all because you had let yourself drift too far from childhood? Or were these foreign lands, colonized through suffering? Could adulthood remain forever *terra incognita*? Would the day come when you laughed like them?

The men's presence electrified Nesrine. She would interrupt their discussions to ask the meaning of a word or answer the most rhetorical of questions. She didn't get their jokes any more than you did, but she still added her childish laughter to the general chorus. The mere idea of laughing with the others was all it took to get her going. Wasn't she adorable?

So life would start later. The here and now was not life but something else: a waiting, a respite, perhaps a drawn-out preparation, but for what? More precisely, what were *you* being prepared for? You had always preferred the company of adults to children your own age. You were in awe of people who never hesitated. The ones whose every action seemed to confirm their grasp on the whole and entire truth. The ones who could with equal aplomb criticize a president, a law, or a soccer team. The ones who could, with a snap of their fingers, answer the thorniest of questions: Palestine, the Muslim Brotherhood, the Aswan Dam, the nationalizations. So that was adulthood, stamping out doubt in every shape and form.

One day it would dawn on you that there were few real adults in the world. That no one ever truly gets over their original fears, adolescent complexes, unfulfilled need to take revenge for their first humiliations. If we still find ourselves surprised when someone we know reacts immaturely, it is naive. There are no childish adults, just children who have reached an age where doubt becomes a source of shame. Children who begin to conform to expectations, stop questioning authority, make confident statements without a quiver of doubt, grow intolerant of difference. Children with raspy voices, white hair, a weakness for alcohol. Years later you would learn to flee such people, at any cost. But back then they fascinated you.

3

Cairo, 1974

Fathers are born to disappear; your own died in his sleep one night.
In his bed, like Nasser, just when everyone was beginning to think he
was immortal. Your mother didn't realize until the next morning. She
rarely woke up before him. Believing he must still be sleeping next to
her, she hadn't dared rouse him. His face in death was as rigidly
impassive as the one he'd worn in life. There was no reason to suspect
he had crossed the threshold. She glanced at her watch. It was after
6 a.m. How strange that he had not woken up at 5:20, per his custom.
At first, she'd worried he would blame her for waking him. Maybe he
just needed a little more sleep than usual? Who was she to know
what was best for her husband, who was a doctor after all? She waited
awhile longer. When still he made no sign of getting up, she worried
instead that she'd be blamed for letting him sleep. She made some
gentle sounds, to no avail. Now sure that she'd be found at fault no
matter what she did, she decided to give him a shake. Against all
odds, this time he did not blame her for anything at all.

The news didn't reach you right away. You had just driven off toward
Mokattam, the plateau in Cairo's far eastern reaches where you were
having a clinic built. You'd taken a day off to oversee the work. Scarcely
had you gotten out of your car when a young boy ran over to you.

'Dr. Tarek! Dr. Tarek! Your father, Dr. Thomas, is dead! You
have to go home right away!'

You would have suspected a bad joke had he not said your name and your father's. You tried asking questions, but his shrugs made it clear that he knew nothing beyond the message he had been sent to deliver. You pulled a few coins from your pocket to thank him before sending him on his way. At the sight of the money, a grin replaced the solemn countenance he had put on for the occasion. You got back on the road, more in shock than grief at the news that had yet to sink in. You rushed to get back to your family.

You came in through the clinic where your father would never again practise, not yet trying to understand the implications of this seismic shift, and took the stairs four at a time to reach your mother's side. You found her sitting in the living room with your aunt Lola. The scene resembled a rehearsal for her new role as widow, held before an audience of one. Visibly thrilled to have front-row seats for your mother's investiture, your aunt showed her appreciation with effusive sobs. You felt almost like you were interrupting.

Sensing your confused presence in the doorway, your mother beckoned you in. Her bracelets jingled with impatience. When you reached her, she stood up, took you in her arms, and offered a commonplace – 'He didn't suffer' – in answer to a question that you hadn't asked. Her face was suitably drawn, her hair tied neatly in place. Since she was a good head shorter than you, you had to hunch your back awkwardly to hold her. For a few seconds you remained still, not entirely sure who was consoling whom. Then she freed herself from your grip and instructed you to go find your sister.

When she saw you walk into the kitchen, Nesrine began sobbing uncontrollably, to the servant's chagrin. For hours now, Fatheya had been conjuring remedies to keep Nesrine from breaking down, from hot drinks to firm embraces and divine beseeching; your arrival was a gust of wind assailing this carefully constructed house of cards. Fatheya gave you an angry look that softened when it struck her that your sister's grief was yours as well. She walked over and looked at you, whispering, 'My dear.' She had a thousand and one ways of saying *my dear*. This one meant *stay strong*. She then nodded her head, to show you that she had a lot to do, and left the two of you alone.

Nesrine's distraught face made her look younger than her twenty-three years. She reminded you of the adolescent girl you used to take for feteer in Zamalek, back when she'd tell you all her problems. You never found one that couldn't be dissolved in the honey of those sweets. Perhaps they were the very thing to bring her comfort at that moment. You wouldn't tell Nesrine where you were taking her, nor would she try to guess; you just had to get both of you away from this house in mourning. She'd crack a smile when she recognized the café storefront. The two of you would think as one, without speaking a single word. She could watch the baker work the dough, sending it spinning through the air above the marble countertop, his expert hand movements multiplied in the mirrors behind him. It would be no more than a misdemeanour against the regime of your shared grief.

You soon chased that thought from your mind. It was hard, under the circumstances, to imagine telling your mother you were heading out for a stroll. None of us is ever wholly what society expects us to be. At that moment, you two were meant to put on dignified faces to evoke respect and compassion. Certainly the picture did not include pastry crumbs in the corners of your mouths, to be wiped off with the haste of greedy children.

Feeling the full weight of your twenty-five years, you sat next to your sister. The chair was still warm from Fatheya's presence.

'You okay?'

In answer she showed you her kohl-streaked cheeks. How could she be okay? She smiled. That was enough.

You had been graced with a moment of calm before the coming storm. News of your father's death would quickly raise a crowd, like sand swept up into the air by the khamaseen of spring. You were too young to have seen Cairo's Levantine community in its heyday, but it was still very much a city within a city. And such a community, close-knit in times of joy and grief, would keenly feel the death of one of its eminent physicians. Your people, known as Shawam in Arabic, were Christians of various eastern confessions come to Egypt by way of Syria, Jordan, or Palestine. They formed the core of your father's practice and your family's social life. Even after generations on the banks of the Nile, many were more fluent in French than in the Arabic they used only when necessary. They were seen as foreigners at worst, 'Egyptianized' at best, a view they did little to dispel.

You were raised in a self-contained and increasingly anachronistic bubble. Your bourgeois world recalled a progressive, cosmopolitan Egypt where diverse communities lived side by side. The Levantines saw themselves in the European education of the Greeks, Italians, and French. Like the Armenians, they had known the ferrous tang of blood preceding exile. This common ground made for strong ties. Your father's family was among those who had fled Damascus during the massacres of 1860. All that remained of that homeland was his first name, a tribute to St. Thomas Gate, where his ancestors had lived, a few pieces of heirloom jewellery, and the pocket watch that never left his side. In the hope that you would one day pass on this heritage to your children, he told you and your sister stories of past times: how successive waves of newcomers spurred the intellectual rebirth of the land that welcomed them, and how during the British 'veiled protectorate' your people rose to eminence in culture, industry, and trade.

While your father's words proclaimed his pride in his origins and gratitude toward his family's adopted nation, notes of melancholy seeped through in his inflection. He knew how much water had passed under the Qasr al-Nil Bridge since those days. Another Egypt had come into being. Galvanized by Nasserian patriotism and dreams of grandeur, it was intent on reclaiming its Arab and Muslim identity. This new Egypt was determined not to lose its elite. Then came the Suez Crisis, the nationalizations, confiscations, emigrations – so many rude awakenings for the Shawam who saw themselves as a bridge spanning East and West.

You remembered a time when not one day went by without some friend announcing their departure for France or Lebanon, Australia or Canada. With no violence but that of inner turmoil, those who left resigned themselves to leaving behind the land they had so dearly loved, where they had expected to be buried one day. You were among the few thousand who stayed. The ones who refused to abandon a country that had turned its back on you, intent on maintaining the illusion of the good life, in their homes and their churches, in the French-language schools they sent their children to and the Greek Catholic cemetery in Old Cairo, where your father would soon be laid to rest.

The next day a crowd gathered at your home in Dokki. One of Fatheya's cousins had come to help manage the procession of mourners your mother greeted with a dignity befitting the solemn occasion. She received the timed visits of those brought to your front door by a mix of propriety and voyeurism. They came with shop-worn phrases of condolence and memories of your father dusted off for the occasion. But all the while they were silently sounding the depths of your despondency. They scrutinized the lines fatigue had traced under your eyes, how your voices quivered when someone spoke the name of the deceased. Then they went off on their way, with a lingering taste of pistachio sweets and duty fulfilled. For some, it seemed, death was life's greatest entertainment.

This was your first intimate acquaintance with bereavement. You came to know the diffuse feeling of being outside yourself, almost dissociated from your own body, as if the mind refused to inflict on the body a pain it could never withstand. You were watching yourself from a distance, replaying each moment: learning of your father's death, welcoming guests, trying to soothe your mother. You could hear each word you said ring out as if spoken by someone else. And you could see yourself alongside Nesrine, whose tears flowed freely while your eyes stayed dry.

It took almost a full week, but then, one night in the solitude of your room, you felt your first tears welling up. From that point on, all you would ever know about your father would reside in memory. But that wasn't the source of the waves of vertigo coursing through you. You were seized by a new distress, the sensation of a responsibility akin to being gripped in a vise. You felt it pressing on your chest. The social obligations that filled the days following your father's death had given you a clear sense of the position he held in the community, the one that would by extension and inheritance now fall to you. In fact, the tears you were crying at that moment were mainly for your own fate. You were an impostor waiting in the wings to dispossess your father of everything, down to the very tears you owed him.

Fuelled by superstition and exhaustion, you imagined your father in the room with you: an invisible, omniscient presence watching your movements and deciphering your thoughts. The moment you felt him nearby, every detail came flooding back: the tone of his parsimonious speech, the expressiveness of his brow, the smell of his tobacco burning in his pipe, the outbursts and cheers that could erupt only during his bridge game, and his ability to count every card played in the round. There was the sure hand with which he had taught you to palpate patients' bodies, track the signs of incipient illness, anticipate the clinical questions that often did little more than confirm the intuition formed at the first auscultation. There was the firm look that had the authority to contain your mother's anger. You briefly wondered whether it was this last element that you would miss the most.

These visions of your father in tableaux of everyday life had a calming effect. His return to his rightful place at the centre of your grief had smothered the flames of guilt that threatened to consume you. Your body settled back into its habitual rhythms. You had thought of him; you had cried. No matter the order in which these two acts had occurred, you had done what a grieving son must. You were physically exhausted but would have been hard-pressed to say why. You wondered how long it would take your mind to extract each of these memories. Before an answer came, you fell asleep.

The following weeks engulfed you in duties and decisions. Your mother threw herself into her new life with painstaking devotion. She accepted the signs of fatigue – what could be more appropriate under the circumstances? – but made sure they could not be construed as giving up. A certain tearfulness was tolerable, despondency under no circumstances pardonable. She traced a fine line between these states and always managed to be on the right side of it. And while everyone praised your mother's strength of character, few noticed Fatheya, who went about selflessly and discreetly fulfilling her employer's many orders.

It must be said that *Fatheya* was not, strictly speaking, her given name. At birth, her parents had named her Nesrine. Your mother soon saw that two Nesrines in the house would sow confusion. And of course it would never do for her progeny to share even a first name with her maid. But when Fatheya turned out to be a hard worker and a quick learner, and was found by careful counting after each service not to covet the family silver, your mother decided not to hold Nesrine/Fatheya's prospective usurpation of her daughter's name against her. She simply, by fiat, gave her maid a new name. Since Fatheya had not been consulted on her original given name, what right had she to protest the arbitrary imposition of this new one? This onomastic redemption only encouraged Fatheya to work harder to satisfy her employer. And at that moment in time, her job was to turn her transition to widowhood into a series of sparkling social occasions.

And how could you blame your mother? You knew full well that her new position was far from enviable. Even a half-century after Huda Sha'arawi cast her veil and mantle into the sea off Alexandria, the right of unmarried women to manage their own lives and administrative existence was a faraway dream. In cases like your mother's, a son was a precious asset. It fell to you to handle the red tape around your father's death, on top of your work taking over his practice. Almost all his patients stayed on with you, despite the great difference in age and reputation.

You continued performing the procedures taught at the prestigious Qasr al-Ayni medical school, which your father had imbued with meaning and substance. Along with technique, he had taught you intuition, to the extent that such things can be taught. How to consider not just a disease but also the person suffering from it. How to listen for not just a heartbeat but also its reason for beating. He was sparing with praise, but you learned to decipher the signs of approval and sometimes even pride that slipped through. After you started off as his assistant, he let you take the lead on more and more patient visits. Sometimes, in front of others, he would even ask your opinion on specific cases or stress the value of your input in his diagnosis. This made you self-conscious until you realized it was his way of positioning you as heir to his knowledge. Now that he was gone, you would have to build your own reputation on the foundation he had laid.

The clinic closed for only two days. It was important to get the practice running again as soon as possible. You had to honour the appointments made prior to his death, and you worked meticulously to decipher your father's handwritten notes in each patient file before they came to you for treatment.

Nesrine got into the habit of coming to see you in your ground-floor office. She knew you'd be working late. You liked when she came to find you there; it made for a pleasant break in the final hours of your busy days. Though she claimed to be there to help, her good intentions never extended beyond the jobs you found for her. After a time, she would get up and make you a 'white coffee' – hot water with a few drops of orange blossom extract and just the right amount of sugar. Night would settle in. The two of you would discuss your childhood memories, or your parents. Sometimes the future, often the past. Nesrine claimed that orange blossom was good for the memory. You never pointed out that she hadn't done any of the jobs she'd ostensibly come to help with. It didn't matter in the end. Her presence sweetened your evenings.

One day you had the bright idea of giving her a cat. She named it Tarboosh. There was no shortage of stray cats on the streets of Cairo, but this one wasn't yet weaned, and looked abandoned. Knowing that your mother would look askance on this new family member's humble roots, you and your sister made up a nobler origin story. Officially, Tarboosh was part of a litter put up for adoption by a friend of yours. Nesrine made a wonderful surrogate mother. She fed Tarboosh with pipettes from your supply closet and petted him more than any cat in Cairo. As time passed, Nesrine kept up her habit of visiting your office, though more and more of her attention was directed toward her beloved cat. This left you free to work on your medical records, while still enjoying her company and of course her white coffees.

4

Cairo, 1981

A Coptic patriarch in the time of the Fatimid Caliphate: you could almost picture him with a fulsome beard, dark vestment, cope, and amice. You could go back one thousand years, you recalled, and still find the Coptic patriarchs wearing the same long beards. The story went on. The Caliph challenged the patriarch to prove that his religion was true. 'Was it not written, *truly I tell you, if you have faith as small as a mustard seed, you can say to this mountain, "Move from here to there," and it will move?*' 'Well,' said the Caliph, 'let's see if it works on Mokattam Mountain!' If it failed, the Coptic people would be annihilated.

The story may have taken place ten centuries earlier, but the tension in the speaker's voice that day was tangible. You loved listening to the people of Mokattam recounting the legends in which they took such pride. Though their settings were now familiar, you had never before heard these stories.

The old cleric was crestfallen. After three days of fasting and prayer, he had a vision of the Virgin Mary. She urged him to go to the marketplace, where a tanner named Simon, who had only one good eye, his left, would come to his aid.

Just one eye? Ever the good doctor, you wondered what had caused this loss of vision. As it transpired, an impure thought had afflicted the shoemaker at the sight of a customer's foot; in an act of penitence, he gouged out his own eye. Even before this compelling evidence of his piety, you couldn't help imagining the scene, and the woman whose sandals would go unrepaired due to this act of self-mutilation. But none of that was the point of the story. For this prudish craftsman was also a miracle worker, a skill that would soon be put to good use. With a few incantations, Mokattam Mountain rose up under the incredulous eyes of the Caliph, who was forced to recognize the truth of Christian scripture.

A silence fell; they were awaiting your reaction. You contrived to look impressed by the ending. You understood how the Copts of Egypt cherished this miracle. In the belief that they owed their very survival to it, they were still here a thousand years later, clinging to the land that today resembled an open-air dump. Everything had changed a few years earlier, when Cairo's governor ordered that the entire city's trash be dumped there. Trucks laden with refuse to thrice their normal height now came to dump their loads. An entire economy arose around the dumps, communities of pickers called zabbaleen, who lived off sorting, reselling, and recycling. They created all manner of things out of nothing, ingeniously transforming soda cans into handbags and even the inhospitable walls of their mountain into a place of worship: for years now they'd been carving the Church of Saint Simon the Tanner right out of the mountainside.

Those who cannot move mountains can at least build a clinic, you told yourself. You kept to yourself the belief that it would do more than a church to help the needy people of Mokattam. In the seven years since your clinic had opened, much had changed. First, a roof had to be built over the original building's four bare walls. What began as a makeshift infirmary now had mostly potable running water and electricity. For years, your weakest patients sat waiting on the folding chairs you carried out at the start of each shift and lined up along the outside wall. Then, you had a waiting room built next to your consulting room. The work had begun last month, and you were thrilled with each visible advance. You even sometimes lent a hand, under the amused stares of the locals, who had never seen a doctor carry bricks. Was that any job for a man of your profession? What physician worth their salt would have time for such lowly tasks? Luckily, these naysayers were no hindrance to your reputation, which had now crossed over from the west bank of the Nile.

You had your reputation and knew just how much of it you owed to your father before you. But the idea of caring for patients in Mokattam had been your own. Fearing how your father might react, you had waited months to tell him. Against all odds, he was positive: pleased to see that medicine was occupying you in your spare time as well, he had simply made sure your new activity wouldn't interfere with your work in the Dokki clinic. After an initial aversion to what she perceived as a waste of time, your mother had fallen into line. There was no shame in learning your craft working with patients of humble station. In case of medical error, the stakes would be much lower.

A noisy, haphazard queue formed each time you opened your clinic, a gathering of the infirm and ailing, toothless seniors, sickly children, and a handful of women who came back, week after week, to ask your advice on all manner of subjects. You pretended not to notice that they were unfailingly well put together and manifestly lacking in symptoms of any ailment that might justify a visit to the doctor. These women's children would be dressed in clean clothes, not the tattered rags they wore for their everyday battles over balls made from old socks in playgrounds strewn with piles of cans and scraps of cloth. In the room where you saw them, you played music, a tape of all your favourite hits from Europe, along with Dalida's song in Arabic, a love letter to her homeland that your patients kept begging to hear. You turned no one away, doing your best to give each patient the care and respectful attention they had come for. At the most, you let those in most urgent need jump the queue. An old man named Mufid began each visit by showing you which of his joints refused to bend that day. Noura would tell you about her asthma, which she blamed on a spell cast by her malicious sister-in-law. Amira feigned a headache, whose sole and recurring cause was the absence of a suitor for her daughter. Perhaps she was counting on your boundless devotion to heal the root cause of this ailment.

Much as Mokattam's zabbaleen breathed new life into whatever objects strayed into their hands, you applied yourself to their mangled bodies, dislocated limbs, and festering sores whose odours were indistinguishable from the slum's fetid air. These strong smells gripped your throat at first, but ceased to bother you in time. They were simply the olfactory dimension of a place you'd grown attached to. You'd long ago stopped counting each case, all the broken ribs and untreated infections and shortnesses of breath. Sometimes you came up against your profession's limitations, when women with bruised faces told you they'd fallen down the stairs at home. You endeavoured to listen to what each one had to say, along with what she didn't. Then you'd escort her helplessly to your office door, where a husband would be waiting. Husbands who came back to haunt you at night as you drifted into sleep. Husbands with hands like staircases.

At times the sight of blood still made you queasy, as it had in your childhood. Once, you must have been fourteen, Nesrine had come home with a badly cut leg after falling off her bike and landing in a prickly pear. She came to you, the soon-to-be eminent physician, for help. Because it was all settled: you were going to follow in your father's footsteps. Your mother lost no opportunity to remind you, perhaps her way of making sure you wouldn't change your mind. Nesrine came to you with a proud face and scraped-up calf. Spines had pierced her leg in multiple locations. She had conscientiously left them in so as not to compromise the clinical case. By coming to you, she also hoped to be spared your father's 'stinging lotion,' and the reprimand sure to accompany it.

But the sight of her wound left you lightheaded. Nesrine had to hold *you* up when you fainted. A decision was made that day. Your father wouldn't let you help treat patients until you finished medical school, a reprieve of more than a decade.

Years later, during complex operations when it was crucial that your hand yield nothing to emotion, you still struggled to mentally dissociate the patient and their body. Even after your long training, you were sickened by the sight of Tarboosh with a dead pigeon in his teeth and that same look of pride as young Nesrine emerging from her prickly pear.

In medical school you discovered a passion for the workings of the nervous system. You would have gladly devoted your life to research, but your father was keen to see your knowledge put to use. You specialized in neurosurgery, and later practised at the American Hospital in Cairo, alongside your work in your father's clinic. He had always viewed knowledge not put into practice as futile at best and suspect at worst. Outside the medical field, he kept a healthy distance from intellectual debates and pursuits. Had he lived to see it, the final months of Sadat's presidency, when many of your university professors and his most politically engaged patients were imprisoned, would have confirmed his intuition. He scrupulously refrained from the slightest moral or political judgment, preferring to stay within the confines of the role society had allotted him: treating bodies. You were never sure whether this reflected a genuine lack of interest or was just a way to avoid controversial subjects in a country where a person's opinions could cost them their life.

5

'Is it a man?'

'No.'

'A woman?'

'Well, yeah … '

'I mean, it could have been Tarboosh!' she laughed. 'So, a woman. Is she famous?'

'No, not at all.'

'Family?'

'Yes.'

'Aunt Lola?'

'You have to ask questions!'

Nesrine ceased to be a thirty-year-old the moment you got going on this game you'd been playing since childhood. She always pretended to be figuring out the rules as she went along. She rephrased her question in mock-formal tones.

'Is the person whose name we're trying to guess Aunt Lola?'

'*Nesrine* … '

'What? It's a question!'

'Usually, one wrong guess and you lose.'

'I've never liked that rule.'

'No. She has more teeth than Aunt Lola.'

'Nonna Rose?'

'Drinks less than Nonna Rose.'

'You call that a clue? That could be anyone! Is she single?'

'Widowed.'

'Aunt Simone!'

'Yes! Brava!'

'Let's do one more!'

You were about to say it was time to go home when the waiter interrupted. Nesrine ordered another mint tea; you weren't thirsty anymore. She'd already correctly guessed your mother, Umm Kulthum, Ronald Reagan, and Fatheya's cousin. Their names were added to the pantheon of personalities your sister had guessed over two decades of Twenty Questions.

'Okay, one more! But I'm warning, you'll never get it.'

Her face lit up.

'Is it a man?'

'No.'

'Alive?'

'Alive.'

'Famous?'

'Not famous.'

'Family?'

'Not at all.'

'Is she pretty?'

'You could say that.'

'That's against the rules! *Yes* or *no*!'

'I've never liked that rule … '

'So she *is* pretty?'

'Well … '

'Ah!'

She listed off nearly every one of her friends, and then moved on to a few of your mother's acquaintances, ironically for the most part, and followed up with one or two female patients from your practice who she'd have liked to see you matched with. That was all she had. Her brain was spinning like a ceiling fan.

'I told you you'd never get it,' you said, with a triumphant smile. 'Come on, it's time to go. Any last guesses?'

She looked resigned.

'No, just tell me. Who is it?'

'Mira.'

'Mira Nakelian?'

'That's right.'

'But we haven't seen her in ten years!' she protested.

'More like fourteen. And that's not against the rules, as far as I remember.'

'And why are you suddenly bringing up Mira Nakelian now?' grumbled Nesrine, who didn't like to lose.

'Because I knew you'd never guess her. And because I ran into her again the other day.'

It was one of those afternoons when one's greatest wish was to become one with the shade of the sycamore trees. An afternoon of accidental sweetness. Of all the questions she'd been pestering you with since leaving the café, only one really mattered.

'I guess she must be married, right?'

'Wrong.'

Nesrine's face lit up. Mira was the first woman you had ever talked about with your sister; she would never again muster such enthusiasm for another. The muezzin was trying to make his call to prayer heard over the laughter of children and throbbing motorcycle engines. You were walking past sand-coloured buildings but had stopped paying attention to your surroundings. It was an afternoon for rediscovering your adolescence.

'What about you? Is there a young man in your life?'

'Come on, Tarek! Don't even joke … '

Nesrine's cheeks flushed the colour of early-spring watermelon flesh. Her reaction surprised you. It was certainly indelicate to imply that an unmarried woman might still be seeing men at thirty years of age. And that brought to mind the inequity of your positions, a thought that evaporated as quickly as it had come.

'I'll have to introduce you to her sometime.'

6

Cairo, 1967

Throughout your adolescence you were a regular at the Gezira Sporting Club. It was a meeting place for the good families of Cairo, at least those whose businesses had not been nationalized. Fear that the club's backrooms might breed conspiracies had led to many revoked membership cards in the Syrian-Lebanese community. As Egypt was swept up in turbulence, your father's profession afforded a peace of mind all the more precious in light of your foreign origins.

Despite her more modest family background, Mira also frequented the club. Her family had been part of the third and last wave of Armenian immigration to Egypt. Her father, Sevan, and later her mother, Karine, arrived as children in the 1920s. Their respective families didn't know each other, but tragedy brings people together, and not only figuratively. In Miṣr al-Qadīma, Old Cairo, where both families settled, the Armenian cemetery filled up less quickly than in the homelands they had left behind. They thanked God daily for this mercy.

Mira's family spoke Armenian at home. They understood Turkish, but refused to utter one word in that language, save to announce the dice roll in the games of tawla that almost invariably ended in Sevan Nakelian's victory. Arabic was used for interactions with native Egyptians. Both of Mira's parents worked at a print shop owned by compatriots, where Sevan rose to manager. Feeling a need to integrate for the time being, though the future remained unknowable, they made sure Mira learned Arabic at school along with French. Unlike most of their compatriots, they'd sent their only daughter to a private religious institution instead of an Armenian school. From an early age, she'd grown accustomed to mixing with friends from more privileged backgrounds, answering the phone when it rang at home and translating the words of the Aznavour songs her parents hummed phonetically.

Mira liked to sit at the club's outdoor tables, reading with one eye on the horse races as the sunlight cast red highlights in her dark hair. At other times she took refuge in the music room, where she could listen to the latest releases from France. Over and over, Mira dropped the needle on Dalida's 'Ciao amore, ciao.' As the Egyptian singer from Shubra who had conquered France sang of impossible loves, Mira's thoughts turned to her own secret crush, Salvatore Adamo, whose records would one day be banned throughout the Arab world. She enjoyed arranging the album covers into tableaux that had the artists exchanging knowing looks, and even invented dialogues and laughed with her friends at the absurdity of their lines. The laughter rising up to her cheekbones gave Mira's face a pleasing roundness.

For you, the club had been a familiar place since childhood. Your father, who had never liked the salons and other literary circles popular in your community, spent his free time in the games rooms. While he met up with his bridge partners, you tried your hand at various sports: swimming, cricket, and even golf on Egypt's oldest course, which had once been reserved for British nationals. You finally settled on tennis, and in time became a strong player. As your new sporting endeavours took you to different areas of the club grounds, you never noticed that each court or field happened to coincide with Mira's chosen reading spots. Only when your fellow players began laughing about this 'coincidence' did you realize she had a thing for you – though she would never admit to this version of the story. Mira, Mira, quite contrary.

It was a Monday morning, and you had to go to class. As you neared the villa gates, you heard excited cries from the street. Traffic had come to a standstill. People were swarming the taxis, which had their windows rolled down and radios turned up. It was almost 9 a.m., and Radio Cairo was proudly reporting that dozens of Israeli planes had been shot down. The tension had been building for days. Levi Eshkol's hesitation, Nasser's self-satisfied invective, the rapprochement between King Hussein and his Arab allies, European inaction, and American prevarication – all had conspired to set the stage for this first explosive act in a glorious new pageant in Egyptian history. In the streets, a spellbound crowd was rejoicing as the news of military exploits reached them, haranguing whoever would listen with the communiqués from the army's high command. Men thrust their arms out of bus windows to clap hands with strangers passing in the street. It was shaping up to be a historic day.

You plunged into the spirited crowd, pushed your way across the bridge to Zamalek, and rushed off toward the Gezira Sporting Club, certain many others would have the same idea. On the club's loudspeakers, normally reserved for sporting results, the radio announced the military support being promised by allied nations. You were swept up in the fervour, buoyed by the jingoistic diatribe. You were only eighteen. It struck you that you might be called up to serve; you tried to push away the thought. As the hours ticked by, nearly a hundred enemy planes were shot down. Your forces were advancing into the Sinai Desert. Commando units had already penetrated Israeli territory.

'I hear Nasser is having lunch in Tel Aviv tomorrow?'

It was the first time you had ever heard Mira's voice. You turned and recognized the reader from the sports fields.

'That's what they say.'

Seized by a boldness you had never before known, you went on. 'And where are *you* having dinner tonight?'

What would be known as the Six-Day War had begun just a few hours earlier, and none could have guessed that, for Egypt and its allies, it was already largely lost. Your army's stories of their imagined exploits thrilled a nation that would need decades to process the repercussions of its defeat. It didn't matter. Everyone around you burned bright with a contrived joy. In a city ablaze with June heat, this late afternoon was mercifully cool. You walked along, light as a grain of sand in the wind, with your arm around Mira's waist. You had a feeling that a day like this gave licence to stray from the strict bounds of propriety.

What did you know about her? No more than she knew about you: next to nothing. You had made plans to meet in Zamalek just a few hours after leaving each other. Hassan Sabry Pasha Street, to be precise, lined with mansions whose architecture advertised the status of the bankers, executives, lawyers, and members of parliament who lived there. You considered this the ideal backdrop for your attempts at seduction.

Only the sight of her finally arriving dispelled your subconscious fear that she would not come. You'd spent the early evening imagining a romantic stroll, leading up to a meal at the elegant restaurant where you had reserved a table. But as soon as you began laying out your plans, Mira stopped you, stating in no uncertain terms that these pretentious avenues did nothing for her. Better, she said, on a historic day like this, to find some bar where the drinks would flow and toasts be raised to Egypt's new-found greatness. Surprised, you gave in without insisting, leaving Mira to choose your destination. She led the way with a smile on her face.

❧

'Do you like dancing?'

It wasn't properly a question, and you had scant evidence on which to base your answer. You stammered a few words, which Mira more or less ignored; in any event they were drowned out by the rush of noise when you opened the door.

Mira was clearly on familiar ground. She greeted the waiters with friendly taps on the shoulder and moved with a natural ease through the garish lighting and loud music. You'd been dragged into the discotheques attached to Cairo's grand hotels before, but they were pictures of innocence next to this place where you now found yourself. You and Mira were standing. You were served a drink you didn't remember ordering. She had already settled up. Mira, Mira, supersonic. Having your drink paid for by a girl you didn't really know would have seemed inconceivable not long ago, but nothing surprised you anymore.

'Do you come here often?'

Mira cupped her hand to her ear to show you she hadn't heard. You moved your mouth up to her face and forced yourself to repeat what now felt like a silly question. She didn't bother answering and grabbed your arm to drag you onto the dance floor. You had never danced before. After spending years learning the steps of medical procedures, you now realized you would have to learn to dance in a matter of seconds. In a desperate search for inspiration, your gaze latched on to the movements of the disorderly crowd. You couldn't tell what it was in your glass but had the feeling a generous swig wouldn't do you wrong.

Two days: in the same time it took enemy forces to capture the Sinai Peninsula, Mira occupied your thoughts. No one saw it coming or put up much of a fight. Two days. The strategy was to slip in under the radar, neutralize all resistance, then proceed to attack. As Leila bewitched Majnun in the fairy tales of your childhood, Mira had so fully taken possession of your mind that you felt her presence all the more sharply when she wasn't with you. Over ten thousand Egyptian soldiers did not return from battle to tell the tale of your nation's defeat, while at home you were living out the final hours of an illusory victory. The euphoria in the city streets was the outward reflection of the ardour inside you.

You saw her the next day, and again the following evening. Every hour apart was spent in that naive bewilderment and agonized apprehension of early infatuation. You slept badly, examined your smile in the mirror from every angle, and reflexively twisted your right wrist, where you wore your watch. You practised dance steps when no one was looking. You also confided in Nesrine, who had never before shown such interest in hearing every last detail of your day. At the tender age of sixteen, she was a self-proclaimed expert in the arts of seduction. Her reading on the subject consisted primarily of the copy of *Madame Bovary* she had pilfered from your mother's library and flipped through in search of spicy passages. Mira maintained that women's hearts were all alike, but unfathomable to a callow male brain such as your own. Who better than her to spearhead your campaign to conquer love? She took charge of your psychological and sartorial preparations for each date, and could be found every morning eagerly awaiting your report, to assess the evening's advance. You could sense your mother in the army general Nesrine had become; it was touching, amusing, and even a little terrifying. She'd pick out your outfits and inspect your gelled hair, alert to the slightest hint of a mutinous tuft. When Mira saw you coming, she'd shrug at your boyish good looks and run her hand through your hair to restore some semblance of freedom.

7

'What do you mean, *didn't show up*? Are you sure you were at the right place?'

'It's been set since Monday ... '

Nesrine was trying to pinpoint the flaw in her plan. She had determined the best meeting place by evaluating a range of hypotheses, mentally plotting out each option on two axes: probability of occurrence versus effectiveness in achieving the desired outcome. She thought she had considered every variable but had to admit that you being stood up was not among them. This was all the more dismaying since this particular date was of great strategic importance, designed to enable her to (tactfully) gather intelligence on which to base her opinion of Mira. One couldn't place blind trust in a girl who had bought you a drink you hadn't ordered, even a member of the Gezira Sporting Club.

'Something must have happened the last time you saw each other! You must have upset her, without realizing it ... '

Nesrine was thinking this over when a flash crossed her eyes.

'Oh, you didn't tell her, did you?'

'No, I didn't say *I love you*.'

You said these words in the tone of a student reciting basic instructions. She looked at you suspiciously, implying she doubted your ability to follow clear instructions, and then broke the silence:

'Then something must have happened to her ... People are crazy these days! I saw an old man nearly trampled to death. By people dancing to folk songs!'

'Well … no, actually.'

'No what?'

'After waiting for over an hour, I went to her house and saw her through the window. She was reading a book in her living room.'

'Wait – you're saying you knew her address?'

'Not exactly … I'd sort of figured it out from her stories, what part of Miṣr al-Qadīma she lived in.'

'Of course! It's so obvious! She let you figure out her address and then purposely didn't come *to see if you'd go find her*! You're so clueless! Can't you see? I'm sure she had three girlfriends staking out the house to see if you'd show up while she pretended to read!'

Nesrine's mind was firing on all cylinders. She'd found the missing piece she needed to set the wheels back in motion. After a few moments' reflection, she decided to tell you what to do next. In a word, nothing. *Nothing?* Yes, nothing. No more dates. You were simply to wait until you ran into Mira, casually, at the club. Affecting indifference would bring her back grovelling. When she realized her scheming had backfired, she would be mortified to the depths of her soul – this was taking it further than you wished to go, but Nesrine seemed convinced that it was necessary. Only then could you consider forgiving Mira.

Energized by this turn of events, Nesrine slammed her fist on the table to signal that her campaign would end in triumph. 'It's a matter of days,' she said with joy, before taking her leave.

After losing ten thousand men, Egypt agreed on the Thursday to a ceasefire in the war that had begun on Monday. And you didn't see Mira again for fourteen years.

8

Cairo, 1982

In that moment alone with her father, she asked him whether he thought she had chosen a good husband. With a tender smile, he replied, 'Almost as good as your mother's.' He was about to add that the only thing this man was missing was three letters at the end of his surname, but refrained. In her wedding dress and jewels, she suspected he would never again broach the subject of her marrying outside the community but nevertheless found peace in his answer. Then she asked him the one question that mattered to her.

'Are you proud of me?'

They stood in the street like a pair of angels who'd lost their way. He was taking pains not to dirty his suit by leaning against the white Mercedes that had just dropped them off; she was struggling to recall how she had imagined this day in her girlhood. She closed her eyes and tried to form an image. Nothing came: neither dress nor decorations, no grand entrance at the church or first dance. Nothing at all. Yet she could have sworn she'd pictured it so many times before. She must have dreamed more of the wedding being over and done with than of the day itself. It felt like a rational explanation. Distracted by her reflection in the glass of the front door, she didn't seek out another. Before long, she was waved into the church.

As the one and only concession made by Mira's mother-in-law, the wedding was held in the Armenian Catholic Cathedral of the

Annunciation. The pews would be filled with the bride's and groom's families and friends, and respected community members who were best included on such occasions. Most of the assembled guests had been invited by her new husband's family. The thought that this imbalance might be noticed weighed on Mira throughout the day, both at the mass, where she sat in the choir facing the guests, and later during the evening reception.

In a wedding gown embroidered with rose petals, Mira looked younger than she was. At Nesrine's behest she wore a floral crown that echoed her outfit and pulled back her auburn-streaked dark hair. She was getting used to the feel of the white gold and diamond wedding ring, purchased from one of the Armenian jewellers Adly Street was famous for.

The flowing wine quelled the uncharitable whisperings of those wondering whether thirty-three wasn't a touch old to be a bride. But the one subject discussed without fail at every table was the bride and groom's reunion. The happenstance of it made the wives swoon and the husbands laugh.

'Just imagine! She leaves him during the Six-Day War and finds him again fourteen years later – on October 6 no less! At the Armed Forces Day Parade!'

The story on everyone's mind and lips had taken place on the eve of Eid. You were sitting in a café, distractedly watching a TV broadcast of the parade commemorating Operation Badr at the start of the Yom Kippur War. In the middle of the military parade, two officers and four soldiers got out of a truck, as if it had broken down. They threw a grenade, then opened fire on the presidential rostrum. These images that would be seen around the world in the coming days sent an electric shock through the café, where you watched them play out live. Customers shrieked in disbelief at the scene unfolding before their eyes. Others hushed them, to better hear the comments of news presenters overtaken as history was written before their eyes. By then, people were packing into the café to watch the TVs or just escape the chaos in the streets, where the frenzied mob mirrored the bloodied masses fleeing the front rows of the national parade. No one heard the man's exalted cry – 'I have killed the Pharaoh!' – drowned out by automatic weapon fire. The announcement soon came: President Sadat had not survived. One sentence pierced the ambient cacophony to reach your ears: a sincerely incredulous question, asked by a long-forgotten voice.

'Tarek, is that you?'

Had it taken a nation thrown off its axis to bring you and Mira together again? Mira, Mira, apocalyptic.

The months leading up to the wedding were spent getting the family home ready for your move. The main job was to reconfigure the second floor of the Dokki villa into a self-contained apartment for you and Mira. The ground floor would house your practice; the third, your mother and sister. Your mother had been hard at work supervising the renovation. In a remarkable feat, for Egypt, it was finished on schedule. Your fiancée handled all questions of decor. Given how little these two women's personalities seemed to predispose them to agreement, it was surprising to see an understanding blossom, one that soon outgrew the bounds of mere cordiality. Your mother had clothed her military discipline in velvet gloves, while her future daughter-in-law walked the line of pragmatism and appeasement. They were dissimilar in every way, down to physical appearance, and you smiled at the sight of Mira thoughtfully eschewing high heels in her presence to minimize their height difference. Both women sensed a complementarity and sincerely respected each other. You were almost jealous of their swift complicity.

To your great relief, you were able to stay out of the renovation. Though you could hear the sounds of the work from your ground-floor clinic, you asked few questions, claiming that you preferred to be surprised. You would wait until the day after your wedding to see the result. In the Armenian tradition, it fell to your wife's mother to welcome you into your new home. She offered you a spoonful of honey with nuts, to wish you a sweet life. The spell lasted barely a year.

9

When you got to Mokattam that evening, a crowd had already gathered in front of the clinic. Though you were forty minutes late, everyone knew you came every Wednesday and would never miss your appointment without notice. As you drove further and further out of central Cairo, you felt a second wind pushing you along and taking your mind off the toils of your twelve-hour day. You parked your car next to the building and before long were hit by the familiar waft of burning garbage. Disdaining even the most basic semblance of a lineup, people rushed over to regale you with their afflictions, only to find themselves outflanked by other, earlier arrivals. With a furtive glance at the crowd, you singled out a few cases that looked especially urgent – young children, elderly or visibly ailing individuals, critical cases – and began consultations. On that sweltering evening, the single fan you normally directed toward your patients was of little help. Your work ran the gamut from general practice medicine to basic health and safety. There were injuries from dangerous building sites and infant malnutrition, and of course the abdominal pains and urinary bleeding that were the classic signs of bilharzia, caused by a lack of clean drinking water. The list went on and on.

To this day, you still sometimes think back on that evening.

You had finished the last patient's medical record and were filing it away in its place in your cabinet, enjoying the relative quiet of the moment. At long last, your open window was letting in a wisp of cool air through the bug screen. You looked out over the rooftops of neighbouring houses, all a single colour thanks to the sand, and your gaze settled for a moment on the lights of Cairo. They seemed to dance before you, pulsing to the faraway rhythms of traffic. You unplugged the fan, closed the window, turned off the light, and headed for the door. Just as you turned the key in the lock, you were startled by a movement from behind your back. You turned around and saw a human form emerging from the shadows. A girl, you thought, before realizing it was a young man. He couldn't have been more than twenty.

He said nothing, but stared at you. Your first reaction was a guarded tension. If it hadn't been so dark, you'd have seen that his gaze expressed not a hint of threat or dominance.

'Can I help you, my boy?'

He bit his lip.

'Are you the doctor?'

His deep, confident voice did not fit his adolescent physique. You nodded and felt all the pressure that had built up inside you releasing, giving way to the fatigue that the end of a long day brings. After making sure the clinic door was locked, you told him that your shift was over but you'd be back next week. That answer didn't satisfy you, and you asked how you might be of service.

'It's my mother … I think you should come see her. She doesn't go out. We live just down the road.'

In his right hand, he held out a few crumpled bills. Nothing in his attitude suggested he was asking you a favour. It felt more like the offer of a boy accustomed to negotiating. While nowhere near the fees charged at your Dokki clinic, he was offering far more than you would have expected from a denizen of Mokattam. At first you suspected the money might be stolen, prey to the prejudice that a banknote in poor hands could only have a suspect origin. How stupid of you; it was more likely the fruit of months of deprivation.

Hoping he hadn't read your mind, you thanked him, made him take back his bills, and showed him to your car.

Just down the road turned out to be a circuitous route of four or five kilometres of winding lanes alternating with semi-paved roads. As you drove, you tried to learn a bit more about his mother's condition. All he would say is that she wasn't crazy.

'No, of course not,' you murmured.

But what did you really know about it? You hoped the future would prove you right. His face gave no further clues; it bore the youthful expression of someone with no interest in social niceties. He said nothing for the rest of the drive, save a series of curt directions. You followed them attentively. He made no attempts to fill the silence beyond a bare minimum. No doubt you were the same at his age.

'It's here,' he said at last.

The house seemed to stand apart from all other dwellings. In places its crooked main walls revealed the shapes of the mud bricks used to build it. Two windows, set in solid wood frames, quite clearly came from different buildings. The second of them was not in use; it seemed to serve mainly as an anchor for the clothesline attached to a post in the yard. A few items of clothing hung drying, awkwardly swaying in the night's dyspneic wind. From inside the house, a woman's voice cried out in surprise at the sound of your car door slamming shut.

'Ali, is that you?'

'Yes, ya ummi. I've brought a visitor,' he answered as he passed through the door.

'At this hour? You should have warned me,' she said, rising from her bed.

In her voice you heard equal parts curiosity and reproach. At the sight of you following behind her son, she softened. She put her veil back over her hair and shook your hand.

'Welcome to my home!'

The home in question had two floors. The front door opened onto a room almost entirely filled by a bed. The rest of the first floor was a second room, which Ali led you into before you had time to introduce yourself.

'He's a doctor. I asked him to come see you.'

He knew full well that this would merit a reproving look.

'We don't need a doctor. And we can't afford one either!' she snapped, staring at her son, before softening and turning to you. 'Besides, this gentleman is far too well-dressed to be working at this hour. Are you thirsty, perhaps? I have a delicious karkade, from Aswan.'

'A karkade would be perfect.'

Ali soon realized that his mother had no intention of allowing herself to be examined, and any attempt to persuade her would be futile. Without betraying the effort it entailed, she walked over to the stove, unhooked a battered saucepan hanging from the wall, and put water on to boil. Other utensils hung from nails sunk haphazardly into the mud bricks that peeked through the peeling paint. Your eyes wandered over the miscellany of objects piled along all four walls, a collection of disparate and worthless items that seemed dedicated less to their original purposes than to masking the bareness of this dwelling. Two or three stacked pails of water, an upturned ceramic basin, wooden sticks of varying lengths, and, at the foot of a staircase, a pile of heavy stones support-ing a makeshift post positioned to support the central beam. You had the feeling you must not lean against it. While the precarious life here on display was no surprise, you had never before experienced it so intimately. The house was built right on the ground, so the dirt floor immediately absorbed the drops of water that the woman's jerky movements involuntarily spilled from the pot. Ali rose to take it from his mother's hands, but she made him sit back down with a look that brooked no protest.

She asked if you were hungry; you were not. She asked if you'd like a plate of foul mudammas; you politely declined. She apologized for not having anything else to offer you; before you could protest again, you found yourself seated in front of a steaming plate of beans. You pretended not to notice that she had served a smaller helping to her son, and an even smaller one to herself. The walls were covered in frames, none of which seemed to line up with the others. A collection of coffee pots hung in front of a mirror just above the stove, in an area also lined with many shelves. One held a tape deck. Music played in the background, Mohamed Mounir. She got up every half-hour or so to flip the tape and missed no opportunity to look at the blue cover in its case. Clearly the singer's broad smile didn't leave her indifferent. Whenever her favourite song came on, she would stop and clap her hands, and when the chorus came around again, she'd sing along: 'Shababeek, Shababeek.' Now and then she'd bang her leg against the table and pretend to laugh at her own clumsiness. Though she must have been around forty, her face was weathered and her hands marked by a life of hard labour. Around forty: too young for the maternal tone she took with you. Sometimes she would repeat certain words after you, not because she didn't know them but to show how much she cared about understanding the meanings you gave them. She was truly interested in what you had to say. You stopped cluttering your sentences with platitudes. Freed from the constraints of propriety, you took time to answer her questions as truthfully as possible. She asked about your childhood, and you couldn't tell whether it was a random choice or a particular fascination. You changed tack, pointing out that you had been talking about yourself for the entire evening, and you knew practically nothing about her. She smiled and dodged.

'It's true. When I'm with the doctor, it should be my job to answer the questions! But you still haven't told me *why* you became a doctor.'

You shrugged as if you'd never thought about it, as if it hadn't really been a choice at all, as if she'd caught you off guard. This triggered a loud laugh that soon proved contagious. She started telling you that it didn't matter, since she didn't know why you were standing there in front of her either, but she was laughing too hard to finish her sentence. So you too laughed, and laughed some more. You asked Ali if he knew what he wanted to be when he grew up. At nineteen, it seemed he'd never considered that he might one day live another life, in which he might do something different than today.

'I think I'd like to heal people, too.'

'Really? One doctor who doesn't know why he became a doctor, and another from Mokattam. I have the best medical team in the world!'

She started laughing again, but you would have sworn it was different this time, as if she were trying to drown out the sound of something breaking inside. She turned over the now-familiar cassette case a few times, and then you saw her covering up an exhausted yawn.

'Is my examination over, Dr. Don't-Know-Why?' she asked, with feigned concern.

She held out her hand, palm open to the sky. You pretended to take her pulse.

'Your examination is over,' you replied with a smile.

'Good thing. I wouldn't want your wife to worry about you being out so late.'

A veil of surprise passed over your eyes. You'd spent the whole evening talking about yourself without once mentioning Mira. With your thumbnail, you worried the ring on your finger. She smiled. You motioned to her not to get up and headed for the door.

Ali walked you to your car. It was a surprisingly mild night, for November. A new gravity coloured his voice, far from the smile he'd worn all evening as you chatted with his mother.

'She was fine tonight … I mean, she isn't always like that.'

'Does she make sudden movements?'

'Yes, and other things, too. Her hands. Sometimes they move by themselves.'

'It could be nothing.'

You hated yourself for this lie. It was most certainly not *nothing*. But at that moment, you wished you could believe it. Maybe you wanted to see him smile one last time before leaving. You tried to alleviate any unease you may have caused.

'I'll come back next week, if you like. After my shift.'

'Thank you, doctor.'

'Thank you both for a nice evening.'

From outside, you saw the light fading from the windows. Ali had gone back to his mother's side. He would sleep across from her, in the main bedroom.

You started the car and eventually found your way home. A plate of breaded schnitzel and sweet potatoes sat waiting on the kitchen table. Everything was cold. You carefully covered it, put it in the fridge, and went upstairs to shower. Though you had grown accustomed to the smells of Mokattam, you thought of this shower as a passage between two worlds. For a long time you stood still under the jet of steaming water, then took a bar of soap and vigorously scrubbed, as if to wash your body clean of all trace of the last few hours. There was the distinctive creak of the faucet shutting off the water. You emerged from the bathroom, slightly dizzy from the heat. Mira, Mira, half-asleep. She was lying in the half-unmade bed. She had left on the light on your side. You kissed her on the shoulder without waking her, then pulled over her the sheet that had slid down. You turned off the lamp and lay down beside her.

10

For no reason you could name, you hadn't told Mira about Ali and his mother. She'd stopped making you dinner on the evenings you worked at the clinic, limiting herself to the wry joke that Mokattam was an ugly name for a mistress. The lingering scent of garbage on your clothes told her you weren't spending your evenings being unfaithful. There were no reproaches, just hints and a disillusioned smile.

You had gotten into the habit of visiting Ali and his mother every time you worked in Mokattam. 'My doctor has arrived,' she would exclaim the moment she saw you get out of your car, and you'd be greeted by the aroma of the dish she had cooked for your visit. One January evening, however, the usual food smells were absent from the house. You knocked on the door and heard Ali's voice shouting from inside.

'Don't come in!'

'Ali? What's the matter?'

'Don't come in, I said!'

'Is it your mother? How is she?'

Silence. You knocked one last time, then decided to go in. What you saw was chilling. It wasn't the first time you had witnessed such a scene, but it was the first time it involved people so close to you. Ali was trying to restrain his mother, who seemed to have been exhausted by violent, uncontrolled convulsions. She was moaning incoherently and seemed oblivious to your presence.

'I told you not to come in!'

'Ali, what's going on?'

'You're the doctor, right? You should know!'

He looked at you with a violence in his eyes that you had never seen before. You approached Ali's mother and wrapped your right arm around her body, which no longer seemed to be animated by human will. With a wave you instructed Ali to move the furniture aside, then grabbed a cushion with your left hand to place against his mother's head to keep her from hitting herself. She gradually calmed down enough to lie down. She was visibly out of breath. You wiped the corners of her mouth and let her drift off into a deep sleep.

Not a word passed between you and Ali for a long time, as if this hard-won silence had to be preserved at any cost. You watched her body rise and fall with each breath, captivated by its steady movement, like the calm swell after a storm. You spoke first.

'Next time it happens, don't try to immobilize her by force. It's better – '

He cut you off.

'Damn it! What's wrong with her?'

'Ali ... '

'You can see she's not well. You come here a lot, right? You can see it? So why won't you tell me anything?'

You didn't know how to explain it. You searched long and hard for an answer.

'Ali, I don't know exactly what disease your mother has. I mean ... it could be any number of things. Do you know if any other family members have had symptoms like this?'

He lowered his eyelids: a *yes*. You took a deep breath.

'What else? Her head, too? Is her thinking slowing down? Any loss of memory?'

He listened, looking straight at you like a condemned man awaiting his sentence. You didn't know what words to use. In the end you just blurted it out.

'There's a good chance it won't get better … I mean, if it is what I think … '

He betrayed no emotion, clenched his jaw. You weren't sure he truly understood. He understood. Maybe he wanted you to stay a little longer, in case she woke up? He didn't want that.

No more words disturbed the night. Just the sounds of chair legs being pushed back, a door opening and closing, a car starting, and the litany of horns in a Cairo that never sleeps. That night you didn't either.

In the following weeks Ali's mother did not have any other spells, not that you witnessed. You never mentioned that January evening, and long afterwards you would wonder whether Ali's mother had even retained a conscious memory of it. You pretended not to notice her involuntary twitches and tics, which were becoming harder to conceal. She also sometimes forgot certain details, but then quickly recovered and laughed at her own infirmity. *We're not getting any younger,* she would say. Or *If you'd known me at your age!* She wasn't even ten years older than you.

One evening you arrived at their home while Ali was still working in town. You realized you had no idea what he did for a living. Surely something to do with selling objects salvaged from the dump, a link in the chain of Mokattam's intricate recycling network. His mother came to greet you with a jovial remark that the doctor was early that evening.

'Good timing: I wanted to talk to you. Come on in!'

She boiled water for your karkade and sat down beside you.

'Listen, I'm not a doctor like you. I never went to university. But I know all too well what I have. I mean, I don't know what it's called, but I've seen my father and one of his sisters go through it. And soon there'll be nothing left to be done. I can't tell you how much longer – maybe a few months, maybe a few years. Not long, in any case. It doesn't scare me, you know. I'm not scared to die. Even the women up the mountain, calling me crazy because I can't control my movements, because I can't carry water without spilling it all over myself – I don't care about any of it. If it didn't hurt Ali, I swear I wouldn't even bother answering them. We're all put on this earth to die, one day. And if we're lucky, before that, get some nice things done. Mektoub: it is written. But that's the problem, you know? Oh, not for me. I've done what I had to do here. I don't know if I accomplished a lot, but let's just say I did my best. Above all I brought Ali into the world. He's everything to me, you know? He's a good boy. The others don't always see it, but he's a good boy. He's honest. You've gotten to know him a little. He looks up to you. A lot. He would have liked to be a doctor like you. Allah have mercy on him! You can't become a doctor when you're born in the trash heap of Mokattam! No, don't interrupt me … '

She seemed to take a moment to consider how best to say what would come next. When she spoke again, her voice had a new gravity.

'I know it's ridiculous. He'll never be a doctor. But I thought he could be your assistant. You could show him things. You give injections, right? Well, he could learn to do that … I don't know, things like that. Wait, let me finish … I know you've already done a lot for us, and I don't even know why you do it. Maybe because your heart is pure – Bless your parents! But I'm asking you, as a favour. I don't even want you to pay him, Tarek. Because I'm sure what he learns will already be a great reward. He needs something to keep his mind occupied. That's important. Do you see what I mean? Soon his life will be full of burdens. Things he has to do for his mother.'

Her words gushed out. She never lowered her eyes, which showed the wounded pride of someone not used to asking for help. You'd known her for months now, and this was the first time she'd addressed you with such gravity. Her distress was sincere, the favour she asked a small one. You agreed to let Ali help you with your duties in Mokattam. In her embrace you felt the same strength she had shown during her attack. Trapped in her arms, you couldn't see her face, but you would have sworn she was crying.

'Promise me you'll take care of him when I'm gone.'

You promised.

You were sitting around the table over steaming plates of boiled taro Ali's mother had sautéed with tomatoes and coriander. The talk was of President Mubarak. He was less handsome than Nasser – 'They're all less handsome than Nasser!' she said decisively, as the two of you sat half-watching the jerky picture on their small TV. Whenever a young man appeared on the screen, you would ask if he was as handsome as Nasser, but she stuck to her guns. Ali came home later than usual that evening; no doubt she'd asked him to let you have a few moments together. He caught you laughing as he pushed open the big door. When he came in, you asked his mother, jokingly:

'What about him, Aunt? Is *he* more handsome than Nasser?'

She pretended to give the question serious thought, languorously looking Ali up and down as if noticing for the first time the fine line of his eyebrows and the sharp contours of his garnet mouth. When she at last answered, it was a solemn pronouncement.

'He may be the only exception!'

'More handsome than Nasser as a young officer?' you pressed on.

'My son,' she answered, 'is more handsome than Nasser ever was, Allah rest his soul, from his first plate of foul to his last whisper! Would you dare to say otherwise?' she asked, one hand raised up and looking falsely offended.

The question took you by surprise. You turned your head in his direction, and he mimicked the affected expression of actors on movie posters. Beneath his casual airs, there was a certain grace in the way his features retained an adolescent charm.

'Your son is very handsome,' you replied.

'Of course he is! When I do something, I do it well. By the way, will you be having dessert?'

She pretended to be unmoved by your compliment, but her face had too many lines to let any emotion slip through unseen. At that moment, it was pride you read between the lines on her forehead. For a few minutes now the aroma of hot milk and cinnamon had been enveloping the room. She opened the oven door, took out a dish, and placed it on the table with a flourish.

'My specialty!'

You burst out laughing when you realized that your dessert was umm Ali, which literally means *Ali's mother*. That moment was bathed in the sweetness of the last log thrown on a fire, with everyone marvelling at the warmth and chasing from their minds any thought of the moment it might stop burning. In the end you asked Ali to come and work as your assistant on your next day at the Mokattam clinic.

'But I don't know how to do anything,' he protested.

'You'll learn. You wanted to learn how to heal people. Well, you have to start somewhere.'

Ali was speechless. His mother pretended to be hearing your proposition for the first time. She turned to you and, without bothering to hear out her son's opinion, accepted the offer.

'It's a deal, Tarek. But not one penny! You teach him, he helps you, and you're even. No need to pay him.'

Then, turning to her son, she said:

'And you, don't just stand there. Thank him!'

11

Ali began assisting you on your days in the Mokattam clinic, and, after, you and he would spend the evening with his mother. He would arrive for work half an hour before you to pick out the most urgent cases in the lineup and invite them into the waiting room, where they could sit while they waited their turn. Ali was a quick learner. He had a nimble touch and rarely needed to be shown a manoeuvre twice before performing it on his own. He weighed patients and took their pulses and temperatures. He was eager to do everything right and never seemed to be bothered by the smells of illness or the sight of a wound. You found yourself repeating the advice and explanations your father had given you when he taught you the trade. At times you even heard yourself echoing his inflections; it was as if, through you, he were refusing to cease to be.

After a few months, it only made sense to have Ali work at your Dokki practice as well. Just as you had honed your own skills assisting your father, Ali would surely develop a feeling for the profession, if only the right conditions were put in place. You started him at once a week, the day before your Mokattam shift. You'd never seen Ali smile so wide.

'With real customers?'

'We say *patients*, Ali. And the people we see in Mokattam are real patients, too, you know. When I see how long they wait, I think they're more "patient" than anyone else!'

'No, I mean *paying* patients.'

He looked at you like a child miffed at being corrected for his phrasing when he knew you had taken his meaning. You felt a little bad as well to have needlessly caused him to lose his smile.

'What does it matter if they pay or not?'

'Well, if they pay, it means they have a choice. And if they choose you, it must mean you're good ... And if you're asking me to work with you there, it must mean you think I'm good enough, too.'

He seemed to hesitate a moment before his last sentence. As if he were afraid to sound silly, or to have misinterpreted your offer. His voice lacked its customary confidence, his gaze lingered unconvincingly on some detail on the floor. You were put in mind of your younger self in your father's office, searching his everyday gestures for the compliment that never came. Ali was talented, it was obvious – how could he doubt it? You wanted to tell him but didn't know how. So you changed the subject.

'Of course, if you take a day off work to come to the office, I'll have to pay you.'

You still didn't know what he did for a living but had deduced from his schedule that he had no boss or regular working hours.

'But, Tarek, we said – '

Knowing what was coming, you pre-empted him.

'What we said with your mother applies to Mokattam. We can't have you working in this office without compensation. And besides, if I pay you, it's because you're good, Ali. Right?'

12

Cairo, 1983

You'd never seen him looking like that before. In a starched shirt with cufflinks, his hair neatly combed down with gel, you hardly recognized the young man from Mokattam. Even more than the outfit, his confidence surprised you.

'Off to meet some girl at Khedivial Opera House? I think she's playing with you, they haven't finished rebuilding it.'

He responded with a smile, impervious to your sarcasm.

'You like it?' he asked.

'Well, it's a little … '

'A little?'

'A little … much. You know that you're going to have to wear your lab coat all day, right?'

You were choosing your words carefully, taking care not to make him feel foolish. You hadn't answered his question. He didn't ask it again.

❧

The day was drawing to a close. The receptionist had finished her shift, leaving only you and Ali in the clinic. You finished some paperwork while he put away equipment in the next room. You recognized the man who had just pushed open the door without knocking.

'Omar bey! To what do we owe the pleasure?'

'Good evening, ya doctur, I'm glad to find you here. I was afraid you'd left.'

This was no mere mortal man but the incarnation of decades of heavy smoking, unchecked eating, and other excesses that had burst into your office. Omar was an old family friend, feared and respected in the cotton trade, where he had made a fortune. His voice had been a familiar presence since your childhood: a harsh, veiled rasping in which each syllable could be heard dragging itself from a morass of guttural debris, without ever fully breaking free. Age had grotesquely exaggerated his every expression; when he put on a serious look, you were reminded of how you had feared him as a child.

'Tarek, I want to talk to you about something important. But it has to stay between us. Do you understand?'

You respectfully lowered your eyes in reply. He continued:

'You know how much I love Dahlya, may God bless our thirty-two years of marriage … '

'Has something happened to her?' you asked with concern.

With the scowl of a man unaccustomed to being interrupted, he dismissed your question and went on.

'Well, I've been making her happy for thirty-two years without complaint. Thanks be to God, our three brilliant, healthy children are the proof. So, yes, perhaps they have inherited her stubbornness. But let's just say they weren't conceived at a qanun concert!'

You were struggling to see where all this was heading, but loath to interrupt a second time.

'Well,' he went on, lowering his voice, 'the thing is … for a little while now … it's not working.'

'Not working?'

'Yes, not working.'

His annoyance at your failure to take his meaning gave you a sense of what the man would be like on his rounds, inspecting his cotton mills, berating some worker for misconstruing his orders.

'It's not working. We're both there. In bed. And it's not working.'

'You mean she doesn't want to?'

'Of course she does! If you only knew … Word of honour, she has a very healthy appetite, and I don't just mean Turkish delight! To anyone who says appetite diminishes with age, I say … No, it's me, Tarek, it's me who's not working … '

'You aren't achieving erection?'

'Well, isn't that just a doctor's trick, to hang terrible words on everything! But yes, it's as you say. So what do you think? Is it serious?'

You were about to answer when Ali cut in, to let you know he had finished. You thanked him from afar, but he took a few steps toward you to offer the two of you a cup of tea before leaving. The old man's face turned pale. A few unintelligible syllables accompanied his nervous gesture of refusal.

'That's kind of you, Ali, but you shouldn't interrupt us. Go on home. We'll meet tomorrow night at the clinic.'

The end of your sentence was covered by the screech of a chair backing up. Omar was already on his feet, angrily gathering up his things.

'Want to know the truth, Tarek? I came to you for advice, like your father before you – but it was a mistake! A mistake, hear me? He would never have accepted such a thing!'

You couldn't see what had so incensed Omar. You tried to reason with him, but nothing worked. He answered your apology with a slam of the door. Ali seemed strangely oblivious to the storm he'd just unleashed.

'I don't know what got into him … I'll call him tomorrow when he's calmed down. He was talking to me about a sensitive subject. You should have been more discreet, you know?'

'Oh, come on. It's obvious there's nothing wrong with him!'

'What's that supposed to mean?'

'There's nothing wrong with him, and he realized it. So he got mad. End of story!'

While he hadn't done anything objectionable, you were still surprised at how casually Ali treated the situation. He didn't seem to realize the consequences this might have on your reputation. Still, you thought it better to teach him a lesson than express annoyance.

'Ali, most of being a doctor is knowing how to listen to people. Physical symptoms sometimes reveal … deeper ills in a patient. So don't jump to conclusions like that.'

'I know what I'm talking about. We know each other.'

'You know each other?' you asked, incredulous at the idea of this textile magnate associating with a boy from Mokattam.

'That's right, I know him, he knows me, we know each other. He's a customer.'

'A customer?'

'Yes. And let's just say that the last time we saw each other, he wasn't suffering from whatever it was he was telling you about. I'm not a brilliant doctor like you, but I don't think he'll find the remedy he needs at the pharmacy.'

You stared at Ali, at a loss for words. If you were trying to convince yourself that this was a joke, his face left no room for doubt. He smiled gleefully at the effect of his revelation.

'You mean you … and him?'

He gave you an exaggerated pout of outrage.

'What, you think you're the only one who palpates people for a living?'

You couldn't contain your laughter any longer. The image of this cotton mogul, feared across the nation, surprised by his lover at the moment he mentioned his impotence, was funnier than the most hilarious nokta in Egypt!

13

From the hurried way he would close up the clinic at the shift's end, you could tell Ali was increasingly eager to get home. Truth be told, you shared his same concerns; there was no need to ask the reason why.

You had quickly given up on dissuading Ali's mother from cooking for you: it was a losing battle. She insisted on receiving you with customary hospitality and judged each evening's success by your number of helpings. 'In Upper Egypt, this is our way,' she repeated like a mantra, though she declined each time you passed her the dish. Her right hand on her throat signalled that she was having trouble swallowing. You didn't insist. Though she had stratagems to hide the progress of her illness, the signs were all around you: in the veil she could no longer tie on her own, in the shards on the floor after sweeping up a dropped plate. She never left the house now, depriving Mokattam's gossips of the cruel pleasure they took in her swaying gait and slurred speech, as if she were drunk. Ali would get annoyed when you went to his house after a shift to find simmering on the stove a dish that must have taken his mother hours to prepare.

'Ya ummi, what have you been doing now? You promised to rest!'

'Don't talk nonsense … The day you hear me promise something stupid like that, it'll be time to start worrying for real!'

Her voice had become a faint murmur, as if she were speaking to herself. Though the flow of her speech had slowed and the words often struggled to emerge, she had lost none of her loquacity. She placed her lips on Ali's forehead. He pouted like an adolescent embarrassed by public displays of maternal affection but let her have her way. She continued, staring into her son's eyes.

'All I can promise is that I'll never stop loving you. By the way, you'll learn that women always keep their promises! That's why we don't give our word for a trifle. Not like you men: you'll say anything to get your way! Except for him, I guess … He seems to be a man of his word, that one.' She pointed at you with her chin, before interrupting herself: 'Come on, let's eat. It's getting cold.'

Her words may have been spoken in jest, but you both knew which promise she meant: your pledge to look after her son if she passed away. You wondered where this emaciated body had found the strength to cook pigeon stuffed with green wheat. Though her memory sometimes faltered, she never forgot the recipes of Upper Egypt. She had prepared a birthday meal for herself. The celebration rang hollow, as you could all feel it would be among her last. She hardly touched her own meal, claimed she always ate too much while she cooked. She no longer had the body of a woman who ate too much.

She was losing weight, and sometimes her memory as well. One morning, she awoke to find a young man in the room. He asked her if everything was all right. She was stunned, more by his surprise than his concern, for there was nothing threatening about this foreign presence. He approached her, put his hand on her back, and asked if she recognized him. Before Ali could finish the question, she had already grasped its meaning. She shook her head. No, she didn't recognize him. When she saw the distraught look in the young man's eyes, she was overcome with pity. Instinctively, she took him in her arms, like a mother consoling her son.

14

Fifteen, maybe twenty. That was the number gathered to accompany the inert body of Ali's mother on her final voyage. The sun went on scorching the earth with supreme indifference. *There is no god but God … and Muhammad is his prophet.* The dust kicked up by shuffling footsteps formed a dense cloud that stuck to damp skin. *There is no God but God …* Ali was one of the four pallbearers lifting the coffin. You didn't know the other three. Drops of sweat beaded on his clean-shaven face, running down his neck and clinging to his jugular. He betrayed no emotion, but each time he swallowed, you thought you could sense his throat constricting with sadness. Or maybe it was sand. The unrelenting racket of Cairo could be heard in the distance. Here was silence, there was noise; there life, here afterlife. Next to the bustle of millions of lives, what is the weight of twenty people gathered? Twenty, maybe fifteen.

Some believe that the soul of the deceased remains with humankind for forty days. Yet for months now she had been in the process of casting off her prematurely worn frame. Ali lifted what remained of the bodily vessel of the woman who had carried him in her womb. The veins on his forehead swelled with effort. You hadn't exchanged a word during the ceremony. At many points you'd tried to meet his gaze, but nothing could stick to it. It slid over the surfaces of things, like the perspiration on his temples.

When it was all over, you offered Ali a ride home. The sun was fading. He accepted with a nod. Your two sets of footsteps were muffled, as you tried not to kick up excess dust on your way to the car. When you opened the door, out came the smell of baking leather. Ali said nothing. You turned the key. The engine coughed and the tape played, picking up where it had left off. The sudden noise made you jump; you shut it off. Ali didn't react. His forehead was pressed up against his window, leaving you a view of his soaked back. His shirt clung to his prominent shoulder blades. You wanted to pierce his silence, take a stab at finding words that might have soothed him. At times, you thought he was asleep, his body abandoned to the bumps of an uneven road. At others, it seemed like he was crying, shyly covering up his sobs. You resented those absurd car horns that kept you from listening to Ali's silence. The display showed 7:12, its glowing numbers like green stick figures contorted at improbable angles. As you climbed up to Mokattam, you could see in the distance the tightly packed columns of cars working their way into Cairo's arteries. To the right, red lights; to the left, white. When you were a child, your father had told you that cars must drive in one lane or the other based on the colour of their lights. You were fascinated by this traffic rule, which produced such beautiful effects at night. Plus what other rule could you name that Cairo's drivers actually followed? How old were you when you finally figured out that every vehicle had white headlights and red tail lights, so the colour indicated only the direction of traffic from your vantage point? What makes our minds latch on to details like these?

You were pulling up to Ali's house. You parked the car in front, a spot you never would have found in the dark had you not known about it. When he didn't react to the cutting of the engine, you lifted your right hand from the gearshift, which had stopped vibrating, and placed it on his shoulder. Your mouth was up close to his ear when you whispered that you had arrived. He turned, eyes wide open. You didn't back away. First a breath. Then, a gentle warmth. His lips were touching yours. Unless it was the other way around. After all, how could I know?

15

A simple, orderly system can turn out to be perfectly unpredictable. *Simple* meaning governed by few variables, *orderly* meaning its actions are wholly known and not subject to the vagaries of chance – yet impossible to predict. Physicists call this paradox 'deterministic chaos.'

Your life was circumscribed by three concentric circles – home, community, and nation. What could be more simple? Your home expected you to perpetuate the family line. The community granted you your father's status in exchange for the illusion of a future. And the nation, in its obsessive quest for stability, demanded that each member worship at the altar of morality and tradition. What could be more orderly? And yet chaos ensued.

On the face of it, the workings of your life remained unchanged. The cogs kept on turning, producing that familiar ticking that numbed the vigilance of those closest to you. But the mechanics of this well-oiled, simple, and orderly system had begun to churn out chaos. You may not yet have fully understood what was happening, but you had a feeling. You knew to keep quiet about the doubts that plagued you and the turmoil they had loosed. You were like a child who seizes a momentary lapse in their parent's attention to open a box of matches. The child doesn't know when exactly it will happen or what kind of fire they will spark. But they understand the possibility, however remote.

Ali had taken a place in the system. There were so many things you pretended not to see: that he was an intruder with one foot in the house, straddling the threshold of a family accessible only through birth or marriage. That he remained ever an impostor to a community separated from him by religion and social status. That the sense of freedom with which he lived life was seen as a threat to the morals of his nation.

All this created an imbalance between you and Ali. You minimized it, perhaps even enjoyed it. Was the frame that society forced you into not a gratifying one? You got to pass on to Ali all you had been taught about medicine. You got to be the one who knew, the one who owned, the one who gave. You put your knowledge within reach of a man who could never possess the same claim to it. He needed you more than you needed him: there was no need to belabour the point. And you made sure this asymmetry was not reflected back to him when you were in each other's presence. Unlike your mother, when she *did good works* – an oblique phrase that left the listener free to imagine the scope of her generosity – you had no thought for glory. You wanted only to keep up appearances, to keep the system unchanged on the surface. Simple, orderly.

But from a single action, chaos springs. That kiss, the previous day. You had read it as a mark of affection from a boy disoriented by his mother's death, a clumsy attempt to show you his attachment and express a need for comfort. But could it be more?

You knew little about homosexuality. It was treated as a joke, a Western perversion, almost never a topic of discussion. There had been one patient, years earlier, who sought your advice on the topic. You hadn't been much help, but you assured him that you wouldn't turn him in. Beyond that, the subject was as absent from your social life as it was from the Egyptian penal code. There were certainly cases of people imprisoned for 'inciting debauchery,' but you would have been hard-pressed to name a homosexual in your circle. There probably weren't any. You wondered whether old Omar fell into the category, and immediately laughed. Unthinkable! He was married. That he should find himself in bed with a male prostitute was more likely a sign of the onset of senility.

Yet you were upset by the image. Omar and Ali together, the worn-out body of the older man paying for the vigour of the younger one. What price did he pay to foist his bodily decay on a young man like Ali?

Ali fascinated you. He lived in a realm of absolute freedom, devoid of calculation, at one with the present. Unlike you, he had no past to bind him and no future to constrain him. He seemed content to simply live; you wished that living like that might be contagious. When you tried to imagine the boy you were at his age, no clear picture emerged. Looking back on your own choices, you were dogged by the thought that you had been methodically deprived of each and every choice life held out to you – by your parents, by social conditioning or fixed habits of thought, by duty or atavism or custom or cowardice. As if there had always been some good reason not to decide for yourself. Did you really believe you could escape the burden of all these decisions simply by evading them? And what was the end result? Had you enjoyed even a hint of the infinite lightness that seemed to fill Ali's lungs with every breath?

And could it be that he liked you that way?

The day before, in your car, when you'd felt his lips on yours, you'd been surprised by their softness. Would it have reassured you to feel an instinctive repulsion instead? There had been nothing of the sort. You'd enjoyed their slightly salty taste. Your heart rate had quickened. You reverted to your teenage self, taking your first sips of alcohol, spurred on by a more daring boy from school.

You recalled your first kiss with Mira. There was the one you'd hoped for in vain as you emerged from adolescence, and there was the one that had materialized fourteen years later, in the entrance-way to her house. She wasn't the first girl you had kissed, and yet the moment your mouths met, you felt a shiver run through you. Desire, anxiety, the smell of the perfume behind her ear, the taste of her lipstick. When she didn't shrink from your embrace, you regained confidence.

'Every time I walk you home, I think: How many years until I see you again … '

Against your lips, hers had stretched into an amused smile.

With Mira there had been a seduction; with Ali, surprise. You regretted the association of ideas that had brought together those two kisses. It was foolish. Mira was your life partner, the woman with whom you would grow old, after bringing into the world children in your image. She had won your heart and your mother's respect; your relationship was unquestioned, universally sanctioned. Mira, Mira, full of grace. You felt bad for putting the previous day's rashness on a level with her. You'd pick her up some flowers on your way home to the apartment tonight.

16

You hadn't expected him to come in to work the next day, but he did. He was punctual, diligent, and showed no emotion. It was hard to believe he'd buried his mother the day before, and equally hard to fathom that you had kissed. You watched apprehensively for any sign of complicity or embarrassment, a look, an allusion to what had happened – all in vain. At the end of the day, you decided to broach the subject.

'You know, about yesterday … '

'Yes, I wanted to talk to you about that. Now that my mother's dead, you don't need to feel bound to keep me on at the clinic.'

'Why would you say that?'

'Promises are for the living, not the dead. You kept yours. If you want me to leave now, there's no problem.'

'Of course not. Not at all … Besides, I wasn't talking about that, I meant about yesterday, when we … '

'Kissed?'

'Yeah, that. The kissing.'

'What about it?'

'Well, you're acting like nothing happened. I wouldn't want you to think that … '

'I don't think anything. I'm used to not recognizing the men I kissed the night before.'

His voice held no hint of aggression, at most a touch of defiance. He spoke in a calm, composed tone as he folded up his things, without rushing any move in any way. He said goodbye with the same detached smile as always.

❧

You never wore cologne to work in Mokattam – both as a courtesy to your patients and because all such efforts were futile where you were going. Yet that evening you found yourself furtively squeezing the atomizer to release a spritz of fragrance. After your conversation with Ali, the following day at work had seemed interminable. The last words you'd exchanged kept racing around in your head. You didn't want to become another one of those men he spoke of without a hint of affect. You thought about it on the road.

No one in Mokattam was unaware that Ali had just lost his mother. Yet many didn't even go through the motions of grieving for a woman they had always and openly held in contempt. Others would offer their condolences, some in the hope of moving a few metres further ahead in the queue he was in charge of. He'd respond with a polite nod that yielded nothing to their manoeuvring.

When you arrived, there were a few patients, as always, who were unhappy with their assigned place in the lineup. They appealed to you as a last resort, and as always you told them you deferred to your assistant's judgment. They grumbled softly and got back in line as you greeted Ali. When night fell at last, and the sick and the suffering had received the rudimentary care you'd come there to give them, you offered Ali a lift home, as was your custom. Would he accept, now that you no longer had the excuse of visiting his mother? You would park your car in the same spot as two days earlier. And then what?

He feigned surprise at your cologne. You felt foolish and blurted out an excuse for this uncharacteristic coquetry. He strolled off with a sardonic smile on his dimpled cheeks. You felt guilty about the thoughts he might imagine you were thinking, the feelings you were projecting onto him, even in this time of mourning. You thought back to his mother and the promise you'd made to look after her son when she was gone. What remained of all your promises? The previous day, Ali had claimed that they were binding only on the living. You glanced out the window: he was lighting a cigarette, leaning against your car.

It's not my place to say what happened that night. I'll never side with those who judge, but at the same time I'll do my best not to imagine it. That part belongs to you, that's all. I'll settle for speculating on how obsession took hold in the days that followed.

Water seeps insidiously into mud brick. It is fascinating to watch: in mere seconds, the first drop stains the material as it is absorbed; then, an entire puddle follows the same capillary path. As the material swells with water to the point of saturation, signs of weakness appear. How long before the entire edifice is imperilled?

You made no attempt to put into words the effect Ali had on you. What good would it do to describe the anguished hope you felt at the sight of his neck, the sudden shiver at the sensation of his warmth, the inner turmoil that preceded each of his words, the uncertainty of tomorrow, or your apprehension that this might one day all come crashing down?

17

Cairo, 1983

Garlic. Clove upon clove, her freshly manicured hands jerkily chopping until the job was done. Garlic and onions, less for their flavour than their aroma. Garlic and onions, simmering on low heat. She had put on an apron so as not to stain her white blouse, a gift from you. Simmering on a low and patient heat. It had to be pungent, to suffuse every room of the villa. She noticed a scratch on one of her nails, and it bothered her. Onion and garlic, chopped and tossed onto the stove, their moisture seeping out until they were reduced to their essence, dried up and withered.

The smell of Mira's cooking wafted down to the office where you saw patients. When she heard you coming up the stairs, she had the impulse to hide her cracked nail. You told her not to wait for you for dinner, and gave her a plausible explanation: having learned that it was Ali's birthday, you didn't feel right leaving him alone just weeks after his mother's death. She could have done without your excuses. You could have told her you had to go out, without the pretext and the guilty look, without saying his name. She would have been spared the need to give you her blessing and the sight of your smile when it was granted. She would have preferred it that way, but she didn't let it show. You were about to go back downstairs when you turned around, sheepishly.

'Would you ... like to come?'

'Enjoy yourselves.'

Mira, Mira, quite laconic. She didn't look at you when she delivered the answer you'd been hoping for. You hadn't noticed the scratched nail that betrayed her manicure, nor any of the others on her hand. You lept down the stairs, heels tapping out the rhythm of your selfish excitement. She wasn't sure whether to add a new coat of polish or strip it all off with acetone.

You gave Ali a nod to show that all was well, and mulled over the choice of restaurant for the occasion. Each one conjured up images of you and Mira. You decided on a barge, seafood on the Nile. Ali hadn't asked where you were taking him. He let himself be led, made no attempt to spoil the surprise. You could feel the anticipation mounting as you drew nearer. He smiled sweetly at your attempts to impress him. He smiled at your smile. He smiled; that was all that mattered. You parked the car upstream. Dining on the Nile: you imagined his face when you came up alongside the dock. How different this must be from all he had known before. The shade of a palm tree further darkened the night. You felt an impulse to take his hand but didn't dare, just a pat on his thigh to show him that you had arrived. As he got out of the car, he signalled his offhand approval.
'Great choice! Their lobster is delicious.'

He had opted for a table by the window. When you asked him to choose the wine, you felt a pang of stress – that it would make him uncomfortable, that he wouldn't want to choose, or didn't drink – but he rose to the occasion, ordering and tasting a Riesling that paired wonderfully with your meal. Under the cover of a tablecloth that almost reached the floor, your leg sought to brush up against his. He waited until the waiter was far enough away before nodding in his direction.
'See that waiter? How he pretends not to recognize me, even though we grew up together. Or nearby, I mean, in Mokattam. You

can grow up next to people without growing up together, I guess. He's my age, but he would never let me play with his ball. His mother was one of the ones who looked down on mine, because their house had one more storey ... And today, he's serving me lobster. He knows I'm not paying for it. He puts his nose in the air. And maybe he envies me. Every time I come here I'm with a different man. Never the same one twice. He's the pride of his family, dressed up like an employee from a good neighbourhood. That suit he has to iron every morning. He probably can't afford a few piastres to send it to the laundries where the boys work the irons with their feet. The pride of his family, yet he's here serving me lobster, apologizing when the kitchen takes longer than normal. He never looks me in the eye when he says sorry, because he knows I never pay the bill. So every time I come, when it's almost time for dessert, I drop my napkin and pretend I can't find it. Then he has to kneel down to give it back to me. He has to look at me. At that moment he despises me even more. No one else in the room has any idea what we're thinking. And when he goes home at the end of the night, he can't get my look out of his head. It makes it even harder to get the garlic butter stains off his white shirt. Leave him a big tip, Tarek. A big tip so he'll forget that we were here together tonight. And be careful, in the future. Cairo's just a huge village. Sometimes a big tip isn't enough.'

His words poured out in an unbroken flow, and without any particular emotion. The longer he spoke, the further your leg moved from his. He had spoken with coldness bordering on cynicism. It didn't seem like Ali, or at least not like the image of him you had built up in your mind. Your joy, grown brittle when you learned he was familiar with the restaurant, was now hacked to pieces by the cleaver of these last remarks, with their hint of reproach and a warning whose tenor you didn't quite grasp. But what bothered you most was being compared to the other men who had brought him here. As if he could read your thoughts, he went on.

'You shouldn't judge them.'

You sat in silence when the waiter brought your food. When he began to describe each dish, you dismissed him with an absent-minded nod. After a few minutes of eating, half-heartedly, you finally asked Ali the question that had long been weighing on your mind.

'Isn't it hard for you?'

'What do you mean? Hard to sell my body? To sleep with men I didn't choose? Old men, dirty men? And fulfill their fantasies? No, that part's fine. It's not hard. What about you? Is it hard to examine incontinent patients? Put your finger in pus-filled wounds? Do you really want me to tell you? What's hard is waiting all night and going home without finding anyone.'

He finished his lobster, which was getting cold; yours sat nearly untouched on your plate. You were so lost in your thoughts you didn't notice that Ali had signalled for the cheque. His napkin had just slipped off his knees. You left a big tip.

Aware that he was the cause of your worried look, Ali smiled as you two left the barge.

'Thanks, Tarek. That place was a good choice.'

Scarcely had he finished his sentence when inspiration struck him. A bus had pulled to a stop a few metres away.

'I bet you almost never take the bus, hey? Let's go!'

He ran toward the vehicle, whose door had just closed, forced his foot into the door handle recess, and pulled himself up onto the roof. He then kneeled on the luggage rack and beckoned to you to join him.

'C'mon! Get up!'

'You're … '

The bus was starting to move. You were struggling to gain a foothold. Ali pulled you up by the arm, amused by your stupefied expression. You flopped onto the roof next to him, lying on your stomach with your hands glued to the metal rack. You'd never seen him laugh like this.

'What seems to be the trouble, doctor?'

'We could have been killed!'

'We could have never met.'

The symphony of honking drowned out your words. At every bump in the poorly paved road, the luggage rack dug into your ribs. Your hands gripped the metal handle like a lifeline. Your heart leapt up against your rib cage. Everything seemed amplified: the city's constant roar, the street lamps' glare, the gas fumes rising from car tailpipes … Caught in nighttime traffic, the bus slowed. Ali said a few words that you couldn't make out, then stood up on the bus roof. He was slowly straightening his knees when you saw him suddenly lose balance. You shouted out his name. He caught himself easily and looked at you like a child proud of his cheeky joke.

'You were worried, hey?'

' … '

'You were worried about me?'

The two of you waited for the last of the passengers to get off before leaping off the roof. Ali went first, pushing smoothly off the high wall of the side. Your trembling legs almost knocked out the driver as he stepped off his bus. Your look of astonishment came as more of a surprise than your presence on his roof; clandestine riders were not uncommon here. Before he had time to glare at you, you slid him a few bills and limped off. You had no idea how much a bus ticket cost.

You didn't recognize this neighbourhood in an unfamiliar part of Cairo. When you caught up with him, Ali tenderly placed his hand on your back. His display of affection could have passed for mere friendship; for a man and woman, it might have drawn disapproving stares. Ali's smile had been stripped of any trace of mockery. You returned it. He took his hand from your shoulder, where it had come to rest, to pull a pack of cigarettes from his pocket. He placed one between his lips and put his hand back in the packet, where a small matchbox was concealed in the folds of the silver paper. He stopped walking, put a match between his thumb and index finger, and ran it along the striker. His hand shielded the tremulous flame he had made and now mastered. He sucked on his cigarette, which lit in two puffs. You watched how this manoeuvre hollowed out his cheeks, how the orange light coloured the veins on his hand. He took another from the pack, without bothering to ask if you wanted one, and repeated the process, this time lighting the second off the first one's incandescent tip. He passed it to you without a word, while twin puffs of smoke issued from his nostrils. You took it, though you had never smoked. The filter retained a moist trace of his lips. You discreetly coughed when you first inhaled.

No one ventures into those dark alleys without knowing where they're going. You matched Ali's unhurried pace in the cool winter air. His hand found in this coolness a pretext to warm up your back with a vigorous rub. You were enjoying the trip too much to worry about the destination. You understood you had arrived when he took a final puff and crushed out the butt on the ground.

Ali pushed open the door of an unmarked establishment. The hum of conversation and clang of metal chairs inside was a shock after the quiet outside. A man behind the counter made eloquent gestures of welcome in lieu of words that would only be lost in the din. He came over to Ali and clapped him on the back warmly, a greeting too effusive to put down to alcohol alone.

'So, who are you bringing us this time?'

'A friend,' Ali answered, with a discreet smile.

'Effendi!' the man said, bowing his head theatrically after giving you a once-over.

With your messy hair and shirt sullied by the roof of a Cairene bus, it was hard to imagine that your appearance justified the honorific, but you received the salutation with a smile. The room was a long hallway with scattered tables. Ali briefly vanished, shouldering his way through the cloud of smoke obscuring your view of the back of the room. For the first time that evening, you had fleeting thoughts of Mira, of the meal she had cooked you in vain, the fact that it was getting late and you had no idea where you were or how you might get back to your car. A coffee cup full of alcohol that you had not ordered pulled you from these thoughts; a second was placed down beside it. You didn't know whether you were supposed to pay right away, but you were given a sign to show that there was no rush. There was no rush at all. Ali came back with his hair somewhat fixed. He traced a circle with his finger, a gesture that meant *Do you like what you see, all this, here?* You liked it here. He smiled. You took a first sip and looked around the room. Two men were kissing on the lips. It was hard enough to imagine any kissing in public in Egypt; you could never have dreamed that you would one day see two men embrace. And it was difficult for you to square this sight with the image of your own lips against Ali's, that first time in your car a few weeks earlier. As if he had read your mind, Ali leaned in. His mouth was moist from the same alcohol, your minds loosened up by your shared drunkenness. You thought of how many nights you'd spend in jail if there was a police raid, and then you thought only of him. Cup followed cup, and at one point you lost count and you had no memory of paying. Your heart beat faster, sending a feverish heat coursing through every limb in your body; a slightly anaesthetic warmth numbed each in turn from its base to its extremity. You put it down to alcohol, but it was something else, a vision of the minutes ahead. You unbuttoned his shirt to put your hand inside it.

At that moment, nothing else mattered: gone were the fear of being recognized, the dread of the fight awaiting when you finally got home, drunk and dirty and far too late. And happy – too happy to realize that there was nothing left of the meal Mira had made you, either in the fridge or in the garbage, too happy to notice the bottle of bleach that would from that night on be a permanent fixture in your washroom.

18

Word spread that a boy of dubious virtue was assisting you in your medical practice. People like talking about 'dubious virtue' to suggest that their own is beyond reproach. It has always been a salutary practice to wash your soul with another person's vice. You couldn't say by which channels this rumour had travelled to reach you, but it bore Omar's signature. The man who had recognized Ali in your office a few weeks earlier was no stranger to the law of the jungle. Those who will not be the hunter soon become the prey. So he fired the first shot. If anyone asked where he got his information, he'd allude to some police connection. Of course a man of Omar's standing had his sources. The idea that he might himself have used the services of the prostitute in question would be too far-fetched to entertain.

For a time, the rumours didn't affect your practice. Regular patients seemed unfazed by the gossip, and new ones came in to satisfy their curiosity while attending to their health. Your appointment book stayed full. It wouldn't last.

Some friends had tried to warn you that people were talking about Ali, without going so far as to report what they were saying. Was this really any place for a zabbal? Couldn't you afford an assistant with medical training? You answered with rational arguments, brushing aside the false motives ascribed to you without addressing their root causes. Yet when they spoke ill of Ali, it was your reputation they smeared. A newly married doctor hires a young male prostitute as his assistant – who wouldn't suspect a double life? Ironically, the rumours weren't false, just premature.

When concrete warning signs appeared, you kept right on turning a blind eye. One patient yanked his arm away at Ali's touch; another asked about his working hours when making an appointment. You ignored it all until, one day, a patient spoke to him with naked scorn.

'Your mother must be so proud of you. Almost a doctor now!'

Ali was livid. You watched him noisily throw down his equipment and roll up the sleeves of his lab coat. His face wore the stormy expression of someone getting ready for a street fight. You had to step in before a punch was thrown. When Ali came to you at the end of the day to tell you he no longer wished to work at your clinic, you exploded. How could he hope to succeed if he lost his temper at the first idiot who crossed his path? Was he willing to throw his future away over an inappropriate remark? You were blind to the truth: it was yours he was trying to protect.

19

As was customary, Fatheya deferred to your wife on matters of household management. So it came as a surprise when she waited until Mira was out to bring up a domestic matter with you.

'The cupboards are almost bare.'

'Do you need money to buy groceries?'

'That would be the third time this week ... '

'Well, if the first two weren't enough, make it a third.'

'The cupboards are emptying so fast! They were full just two days ago, and ... '

'What do you want me to say? We're not short of money, if that's what you're worried about! Here – '

You started taking your wallet from your pocket. Fatheya made a move to show that wasn't what she'd had in mind and tried a different tack.

'I wouldn't want to be accused of taking food.'

'Nobody's accusing you of anything.'

'I was worried about – '

'No one else is worried!'

She paused, then answered curtly. 'Maybe that's the problem.'

For some time now, the last-minute cancellations had been multiplying, so your workday ended earlier than usual. You went back up to the apartment and, thinking you were alone, decided to have a whisky. As you poured out a glass, you heard a noise coming from the bathroom. You put your ear to the ground to confirm your intuition: it was vomiting.

'Mira, are you okay?'

The noise stopped. You called her name again. She answered at last.

'Sure, I'm fine. The cream must have curdled. It'll pass.'

'Are you sure? Want me to come take a look?'

'I told you I'm fine. Thanks for asking … '

You didn't insist. Her last three words smacked of reproach laced with irony.

Mira stayed in the bathroom a long time, then took a shower before coming out. As she opened the door, a cloud of steam emerged, and with it drafts of bleach and shampoo. Nodding absent-mindedly when you asked if she was feeling better, Mira fell into a silence that she would not break until the next day, when you were about to go downstairs to work. She had to get out of Cairo, she said. To get some rest. From then on, you would hear these words over and over at regular intervals. Mira, Mira, metronomic.

That first time, she spent two weeks by the Red Sea. You didn't try to convince her to stay or understand what she meant by *rest*. Was she hoping you'd ask to go with her? The question had crossed your mind, but after a while you'd given up trying to answer it. Later, she would vary her destinations. Sometimes she forgot to say where she was going. She would simply announce she was leaving again, or let you know by other means. Her suitcase laid out in the middle of the bedroom meant she wouldn't be there when you got home in the evening. No reproach, no aggression.

Though your conscious mind refused to acknowledge the fact, her reasons for leaving were obvious enough. The repeated incidents at your practice had become the talk of the Levantine community. There was no way Mira could have escaped noticing. But would she go so far as to suspect your affair with Ali? What goes unsaid does not exist, and it was in neither of your interests for this situation to exist. Only veiled hints disturbed the cautious silence you maintained. You couldn't tell whether these were intentional or mere figments of your imagination. She had stopped going to the Sporting Club, where she once spent many of her afternoons. She had stopped dragging you along on those social outings you'd never enjoyed anyway. She no longer entertained at home. Each of these clues was insignificant, in isolation. You made no attempt to piece them together.

A phone call or postcard in the mailbox would inform you that Mira was on a retreat in the Sinai Peninsula or enjoying the waters at Marsa Matruh. Sometimes a few days went by without word from her, but she always stayed in touch. Above all, she never came home without telling you, an unspoken arrangement that suited you both.

Against all odds, Mira's travels brought you closer together. While her departures were often preceded by tensions, each homecoming brought you happiness. She didn't come back until she felt better, and you always ended up missing her. The two of you got into the habit of celebrating her returns. It was a ritual of sorts, the reunion of two lovers. You'd try to surprise her with a candlelight meal you'd cook for her at home, or the bustle of a Cairo night you rediscovered together. You were never caught unprepared, and she never made the excuse of being tired from her travels. The magic lasted a night and sometimes spilled over into subsequent days before the pall of routine took hold again. Each time marked the beginning of a new cycle that lasted several weeks until she disappeared again. You sometimes thought back to that day in June

1967, how just as you were getting to know each other Mira had vanished without a word. Could it happen again? Would it again take almost fifteen years for her to come back? Or might she simply not come back at all? She told you she needed these getaways to find herself again. And you understood that she needed those moments of homecoming to reconnect with you.

Mira had been away for two days, on her latest trip. Ali was working with you at the clinic, as usual. You waited until the last patient had left before inviting him to stay the night. You chose your words and calculated your timing to make it look like no big deal. As you asked the question, you were surprised by the unusually high pitch of your voice. Ali pretended not to notice. Yes, he would stay. A tacit agreement arose between the two of you, one you renewed daily. By day, Ali's hands were an extension of your own on your patients' bodies; at night, his body was an extension of yours, under your impatient hands. He was there when you woke up. He was there again at bedtime. At one point you stopped asking if he wanted a ride home after your Wednesday shift. Neither of you noticed the oversight.

One evening, when you had gone up ahead of him to your apartment, you saw Ali come up from the clinic, looking worried.
    'I just answered a call. A man who wanted to talk to you … '
    'An emergency?'
    'No, no. Someone who wanted to buy the Mokattam clinic.'
    'Buy the clinic? You told him it wasn't for sale, I hope?'
    'He didn't leave his name, just a phone number.'
    'Probably just some joker. It happens sometimes. No need to make that face.'

Your smile didn't seem to reassure him. He went on.

'He told me not to worry, that I could keep on working there – if I renounced sin … To tell the truth, I was suspicious from the start. The moment he said, "Peace be upon you … "'

The shadow that darkened Ali's expression now spread to your face as well. Egyptians weren't in the habit of using language like that on the phone. It sounded more like a Saudi greeting.

Egyptians had been coming back from the Gulf in droves since the end of the Sadat era. They had been lured by higher wages and free housing to provide cheap labour in a region booming from the oil crisis, and now they returned with VCRs under their arms and much longer beards than when they left. Many had also brought back their new country's religious fervour. Some had adopted Salafi customs; others embraced the political Islamism of the Muslim Brotherhood, whose charitable works thrived in the ruins of economic liberalism. As the Egyptian state hospital system collapsed to the point where it could no longer provide adequate equipment and medicine, Islamic organizations set up a parallel health system with affordable care. No doubt they were now looking to convert your clinic into an Islamic one. In a Christian neighbourhood, that felt more like provocation than charity. Ali must have come to the same conclusion.

If you renounce sin. It sounded like a threat. But what did it mean? How had he taken it? You gazed at Ali for a long while. He was standing right in front of you but seemed elsewhere. He didn't speak, looked serious and agitated. Your concern evaporated; his alone mattered. You didn't like to see his features harden. For the moment, you didn't care about anything else.

❧

As strong alcohol breaks down inhibitions, the caution of the early days wore off. You still forbade Fatheya from cleaning your apartment when Mira was away, but stopped bothering to avoid the door in full view of your mother's window, or to watch for the lights to go out, or to be wary of how far your voices might carry, or to consider whether the curtains were thick enough to hide your embraces. Nesrine used to visit you when you were doing paperwork. That first evening you pretended not to hear her knock, waiting in silence until she went back up to her upper-floor apartment and then breaking out in adolescent giggles once the danger had passed. She didn't come back the next day, or the following one.

Mira had left you a phone number. You called once in a while, less to check on her than to gauge the imminence of her return. You'd answer her questions with banalities far removed from the life you were leading in her absence. And you would finish each call by saying that you missed each other. For her, it was a question; for you, an alibi.

Unnoticed by you, a sorrow had taken your place at Mira's side, an uncharacteristic melancholy that would never desert her. Should she make a permanent space for this new companion or would it, too, tire of her in time? With the passing weeks, Mira came to understand that from now on this vague sorrow would always have a hold on her, applying pressure to remind her of its presence when she least expected it. Mira, Mira, neurasthenic.

20

The TV cables jumbled across the floor tripped Ali as he walked toward the bed. He just barely kept his footing, and swore. You were touched by the sight: this man who could always be counted on to show the same detached assurance, his pride injured by a silly cable. You preferred to get out ahead of the rebuke you could feel coming on.

'I have to find time to disentangle this mess.'

'To what?'

'Untangle it, if you'd rather.'

'It's not that I'd "rather." It's just easier. There's no need to constantly show off all the complicated words you know.'

Overreaction is deaf to reason, so you ran your hand through his hair and tried creating a diversion.

'*Entanglement* is a nice word, though, right? And since you love complicated things so much, did you know that photons can be entangled, too?'

He rolled his eyes, as if to point out that quantum physics wasn't part of the curriculum in Mokattam. You didn't even notice, and went on.

'Photons are tiny little particles ... Apparently, once two photons have interacted at any point in their existence, they stay connected forever. So when you manipulate one, the other is immediately changed in the same way. Instantly. It's as if one knows exactly what the other is experiencing, at the very moment it's experiencing it, without receiving the slightest signal from it – even thousands of kilometres apart! Can you believe it? They're linked forever. Intertwined, even if they can't communicate. Who knows, maybe you and I are like two entangled photons.'

'What are you talking about?'

'I just mean that, maybe if we were separated one day, we'd go on feeling the same things, at the same times.'

Can anyone truly know what causes storms to rage? Ali exploded with a violence that drew his muscles taut.

'Cut the crap, Tarek! What are you talking about? Just because we're fucking doesn't mean you get to say stuff like that. What? Why are you looking at me like that? I shouldn't say *fucking*, is that it? What should I say? We're *making love*? That doesn't mean anything either! My customers pay to fuck me. Or for me to fuck them. Not to make love. If I had to sit around waiting to hear about how we *made love*, I'd never see a piastre. Believe me!'

His chest was heaving, his breathing erratic. You followed the movement with your eyes, watching for a lull in the breathing while avoiding the danger of your eyes meeting. Then you asked him outright.

'Do you love me?'

'I don't know. It doesn't mean anything anyway. I mean … I could say yes and really believe it. And you might answer the same. But even if we used the same words, it wouldn't mean the same thing. Because we've been sweating in bed together, that makes us like your particles? Nah, I don't think so! And when we break up, I can't see how we'll be feeling the same things either. You'll go on being a big-shot doctor, with plenty of money. And I'll keep getting by the best I can.'

'What's money got to do with it?'

'It's *all* about money, Tarek. Everything's about money! Every time someone talks, they're talking about money. Only someone who's never gone without could fail to see it! The world doesn't work the way you wish it did. What do you think? That you can dress me up in scrubs and that makes me a nurse? That all the gossip will go away because you tell your friends I'm talented? That your wife doesn't see? Open your eyes, damn it!'

The sneer on Ali's face when he spit out that last sentence seemed to wipe away the last trace of his youth. He left the room and gathered up his things. You tried to make him stay with a few stammered phrases. Not one word slipped through Ali's clenched jaw in answer.

※

You hadn't had dinner with your mother and sister in a long time. When Mira started periodically going away, you'd gotten in the habit of going up to their floor at the end of the day to share their evening meal. The atmosphere was pleasant: you and your family would make small talk, eat Fatheya's cooking, and listen to the tapes from France.

'What's playing tonight? Another "French" singer from Egypt?'
'Good idea, I'll put on Demis Roussos. It's been a long time!'
'Is he Egyptian, too?'
'Yes! A Greek from Alexandria, like Moustaki.'
'Well, I guess every French singer is Egyptian.'
'It's true: Richard Anthony, Guy Béart, Claude François … '
'Dalida!'
'France is noble, ya habibi. In that country they know talent when they see it, no matter who has it.'

Between courses, your mother would try to extract information about the ailments of your patients, many of whom were acquaintances of long standing. With the excuse of confidentiality, you took pleasure in letting her keep fishing. Her curiosity was insatiable.

Eventually, for lack of anything better to talk about, she'd fall back on the story of her most recent card game.

But your last dinner together had grown heated. You'd been unable to answer Nesrine's question about Mira's whereabouts, and your mother had used this innocuous question as a springboard for a sermon. What could you say about a couple whose husband let his wife travel alone and didn't even know where she was? You told her to mind her own business and went back downstairs without finishing your meal. Later, when Ali secretly moved in with you, that quarrel was a godsend: you no longer had to justify your absence at dinner. Now that he was gone, you decided to turn up with a bouquet of roses, as a show of goodwill. As you stepped through the door, you found your mother sitting in the living room with Omar. When he saw you enter, he left without a glance in your direction.

'What's that man doing here?'

'Oh, now I have to keep you posted on who I'm spending time with?'

She glared at you. Disconcerted, you handed her the flowers, as if they'd been the reason for your visit, and walked right out the door.

21

In the beginning, God created the heavens and the earth. So before the beginning was nothing, nothing but God. *Almost* nothing. To relieve the divine boredom that must have reached back long before the beginning, God created humankind in his own image, an idea that came to him after days of continual fulguration. A generous demiurge, God gave humans dominion over the fish of the sea, and the fowl and the cattle, and well nigh everything else. None of this was much cause for concern since humanity, made in God's image, could be expected to be a good steward. God had merely replaced the nothingness around him with *something*, and before a week had passed he delegated away its management. Then, prey to a fleeting bout of self-satisfaction, God deemed all this creation *good*. But humankind took a liking to its new job. Perhaps fearing it might be challenged, it set about making its status irrefutable. And so humanity, in turn, created God. In *its* own image.

If, in this scriptural cosmogony, the primary task of every human being is to control their surroundings, it has to be admitted that some have done so to admirable effect. Omar built up a flourishing empire of cotton; your mother masterfully played her cards to secure her station in life. Each pursued their own goals: money or power, influence or sex ... But what were *you* trying to attain? Did you even know? And why did it seem so easy to identify in others that which you could not locate in your own self?

You hadn't seen Ali since your fight. For the first time, he didn't show up for work at either the Dokki or the Mokattam clinic. You hadn't wished to visit his house. Out of pride, no doubt, but fear as well: the fear that he wouldn't open his door to you, the fear that he wouldn't be home at all, and of course fear of the jealousy that would sweep over you at the thought he might be at one of his customers' homes. Your sense of order had been thrown off orbit, and so had your mind. You knew no name for this urge that had you in its thrall.

Mira was getting ready to come home. She had called, as usual, the day before to warn you, but this time you were caught off guard. Him evaporating, her reappearing; it was dizzying. You asked Fatheya to pick up a meal from the caterer to celebrate your wife's return and to meticulously tidy everything. She got to work and, as she was about to leave, she placed a few belongings that were not yours on the table. They were Ali's, left behind in his hurried departure. A first. You felt a sudden anxiety about what might have happened if Mira had stumbled on these things. You threw the compromising items into a plastic bag and took it down to the ground-floor clinic.

Although she'd told you not to wait up, you'd made a point of welcoming your wife. She arrived late in the evening. When you spotted her on the doorstep, you rushed to give her a hug. Surprised and charmed, she kissed you back. As she put away her clothes, the smell of stuffed grape leaves drifted up from the kitchen. This semblance of normalcy was comforting. You felt like a patient about to learn that the tumour you'd discovered was, after all, benign.

When he finally came back to work, you hadn't seen Ali for a week. Like him, you acted as if nothing had happened. You demanded no explanation, and he offered none. When you went back up to your apartment that evening, you were preoccupied. You stared at the walls, as if keeping watch on a blackmailer. It felt as if each piece of furniture were conspiring to betray you. Four days later, Mira announced a new trip. Perhaps she could sense your troubles. Mira, Mira, telepathic.

A new distance had taken hold between you and Ali. He came back to stay with you on the night of Mira's departure, but something in him had changed: a listlessness in his gaze, a dullness in his smile, off-the-cuff comments about your lifestyle or the way you threw away leftover food like one who had clearly never known hunger. It wasn't a reproach, exactly, but a reminder of the chasm between you, an original difference. Like oil and water: you may think they're mixing if you shake hard enough, but in time each flows back to its rightful place. Inevitably, one dominates the other. Ali drizzled olive oil over a dish of fava beans as he said these words, seasoning his false detachment with a dash of provocation. You were well aware that he was weighing every word. With a smile, you tried to make light of his comments. A shake of the head to chase an absurd thought. Today, you can see just how right he was. The small but telling details Ali was pointing out were symptoms of much larger ones. You were separated by nearly fifteen years of life, not to mention education, profession, family, status, religion … In the end, you had nothing in common, save that you were two men in Egypt, in a dying twentieth century. And it was this one shared trait, not your myriad differences, that would be your undoing.

You were a thousand miles away from such considerations when you opened your eyes that night. You were aware that you were awake, but tried not to stir your limbs from their drowsy heaviness, so as to not jeopardize your chances of getting back to sleep. In that state of mental numbness, you glanced at the left side of the bed, expecting to see Mira's silhouette, lost in some dream she would surely tell you about later. Instead, you saw Ali's body. He was sleeping peacefully. You'd forgotten. Forgotten that he was sleeping there, just as he had the night before and the day before that one, and the one before that as well; sleeping in the bed where you and Mira were trying to conceive a child. He was lying in the exact spot where she usually slept. You could not now find the treacherous path back to sleep. You stared uncomprehending at this other body that had twisted and turned until your sheets barely covered him. He was lying on his stomach, his head facing yours. Rays of early summer morning sun flickered along his spine. In the horizontal light, each vertebra cast long shadows that joined when his breathing caused his back to rise, and then fell back into place as the air flowed out through his nostrils. His body surrendered as peacefully as if this place had been his own. As if there were nothing astonishing in this flagrant imposture.

Each person carries the seeds of their own destruction. You thought of Nesrine, sleeping on the floor above. Of your mother, invisible sentinel watching over the entire building. Of the window letting the light of dawn shine in on Ali's tranquil body. Of his belongings, scattered through the house; of his scent all around. You felt a tension gripping you, with no way to know whether your quickening heart rate was its cause or its consequence. A desperate pounding. A thundering inside. How could he not hear it? You put a clammy hand on his shoulder. He awoke with a gentle shudder. With half-closed eyes, he read the time on Mira's clock.

'What are you ... Are you okay? You're making a crazy face!'
'You have to go ... '

He got up. Dressed. Gathered his things in silence. When he finished, he glanced in your direction. For years to come you would struggle to parse the meaning of that expression. Right then, you could not utter another word.

22

Rumour. Invisible as the wind in the palm trees, it spreads, sullying whatever it cannot understand. Your office windows had been broken from outside. *Condemning whatever it cannot understand.* You suspected a burglary at first, but nothing of value had been taken. Your furniture had been slashed, your armoires pushed over, your files scattered. *Casting aside what it cannot understand.* There was no mistaking it: the goal was destruction. How many had been involved? Five? Twenty? And who were they? *Shifting shape as it passes from ear to the mouth.* A smell of gasoline, as if someone had planned to set the place on fire. Why, then, had they stopped short? Had they run out of time? Or did it merely make the effect more powerful? Because they would have preferred that you be inside? *Twisting mouths into sneers, passing on information with feigned indignation and a knowing smile.* Your thoughts turned immediately to Mira. Where was she at that moment? And your mother? And Nesrine? Would they have attacked women? *Wallowing in its own certainties.* And Ali? *Hiding its ugliness behind masks: propriety, tradition, morality, principles.* A shiver of rage flashed through you at that moment, of an intensity unmatched as long as you lived. *Rumour, smearing all it touches, splashing indiscriminately.* Where the hell was Ali? *Abhorring otherness.* You left your office screaming. *Pointing fingers, asphyxiating, stoning, immolating.* Then you saw the dead body of your cat, Tarboosh, nailed to a wall. Blood dripped down his unjointed paw, tracing irregular purple lines that ended in the tortured animal's pool of vomit. *Glorying in its own ignorance.*

Tarboosh … How long had your cat spent in agony in this grue-some *mise en scène*? *The beast that feeds on hatred.* A message had been written on the wall. 'He'll be waiting for you in hell.' *Rumour that kills.*

A rapture of flies was already gorging on Tarboosh's corpse. You tried to pry his still-warm body from the wall. Exercising a pointless precaution, as if some portion of suffering might yet be spared him. You must have cut your fingers pulling out the nails; there was no telling where his blood ended and yours began. You, whose hands knew only how to care for the living, could at that moment have slit the throats of a hundred men if they stood in your way. All were guilty.

You had to act quickly. You wanted to make sure your loved ones were safe. You covered your cat's body with a towel and took the stairs four at a time, calling out your sister's name. Nesrine seemed to be stirring from a sleep that not even a ransacking could disrupt. She recoiled at the sight of you coming toward her, with your bloody shirt and wide eyes. You were yelling. You just wanted to ask if everything was all right, but the words you bellowed out were shattered almost beyond intelligibility. You could see in her eyes that you were scaring her. You caught your breath and made a concerted effort to speak as clearly as you could.

'Where's Maman?'

'Tarek, what's wrong? Are you hurt?'

You simply repeated your question, trying to mask any impatience.

'She's in her room, Tarek, where else? My God, what have you done to yourself?'

She began unbuttoning your shirt to try to find the source of the blood. She couldn't find a wound. You couldn't explain. You just sat, exhausted and helpless.

'Tarek, are you going to tell me what's going on?'

'Mira. I want to talk to Mira … '

Mira was in Alexandria. Nesrine had talked to her on the phone the day before. She could well be swimming at Montaza by now. Should we send someone to the beach, to give her a message? No, there was no need. You didn't answer any other questions. Your one care now was to find Ali.

23

The doorbell rang; she opened. The person spoke; she answered. The exchange was brief. She closed the door, looked through the peephole, and watched her interlocutor walk away with his back to her. When he was at a safe distance, she took a few steps into the hall. She met her own eye, distractedly, in the small mirror on the wall in the entrance. A shadow was cast across her sagging cheeks. She did not fix her hair.

It was your day in the surgery ward of the American Hospital, and your mother knew she had time to spare before you got home, enough to figure out the best way to break the news to you. For now, she felt a pain pressing in on her head, like a clamp. She headed for the kitchen, opened the fridge, and took out a tub of water in which three leeches had been languishing. They'd been waiting two months for this migraine.

'Where's the body? I want to see the body. I want to see what they've done to him!'

'Will you calm down? I'm telling you, he drowned.'

'I want to see the body!'

'They buried him … '

How could Ali have drowned? He was just twenty, so physically strong and mentally sharp … You clenched your jaw, as if to stop yourself from screaming more.

'They can dig him up! Since when is there such a rush to bury the first Mokattam orphan who drowns? Who gave the order?'

'I did. I asked for him to be put in a mass grave, when I got the news. He was our employee, a boy with no family. But Holy Communion! What do you want me to – '

'Stuff your Holy Communion! What right did you have? To order the burial of that body without … '

You had never before spoken to your mother like that. Nor had anyone else, for that matter. She replied in an icy tone, enunciating each and every syllable.

'Without being able to see him one last time?'

'Without being able to examine him, damn it!'

'Tarek, I'm starting to believe it's all true, what they've been saying. Be a man for once! We don't dig up the dead, and we don't – '

'Don't what?'

'Don't do things like that, when you're a man!'

'Don't tell me to be a man ever again. You hear?'

'If only I'd told you more often.'

Your mother shouted these last words through the door you'd just slammed.

To see his body, to understand. You suddenly thought of the phrase written on the wall next to Tarboosh's body. *He'll be waiting for you in hell.* What if they meant Ali, not your cat? Had he been beaten to death before they threw him into the Nile? There would be bruising, and you'd have to prove there was no water in his lungs. Had he been thrown into the river, weighted and shackled, left to drown? If so, you would find evidence of binding around his wrists. To see his body, perhaps find some trace of life that might have survived all this. Some dying but not quite dead ember that could be made to flame up again, with enough breath. To see him. To understand. His body. One last time.

You went to the local public health authority near your home, in the hope Ali's death might have been registered there. The procedure was familiar from your work as a doctor. After waiting more than an hour, you were asked for Ali's identification. You didn't have it. It was nearly 5 p.m., and the clerk across the desk seemed disinclined to make an exception so close to closing time. Your mounting impatience seemed only to further sap his motivation. You raised your voice. He realized he wasn't going to get rid of you so easily and reluctantly agreed to take a look. He flipped to the first page in each cardboard folder from what appeared to be that day's stack. To no avail.

'What do you mean, *nothing*? What does that mean?'

'It could mean his death was reported to another office. Or that the information is not yet up-to-date. It can take up to twenty-four hours to update the file. Or that his name was entered incorrectly. Or that he is one of the twenty-seven unidentified dead of the day. Or – '

'How am I supposed to find out where he is now?'

'Well, you could always try the Mogamma. But without ID papers ... '

His last words served to remind you that the favour he had done you was still awaiting its reward and that your chances of getting your information were virtually nil. Directing an Egyptian to the Mogamma was tantamount to sending them to the devil. Seeking information in that Stalinist palace of bureaucracy on Tahrir Square, populated by tens of thousands of civil servants who were all but guaranteed to have no answer to any question you might ask, was the surest way to permanently bog down even the simplest administrative request. You'd been there just the week before to fill out some papers that had disappeared when your clinic was ransacked, and you weren't holding out much hope of seeing them again for several months. You left without tipping the man at the desk, ignoring the salvo of curses that followed you out. You considered asking your mother if she knew which pit Ali had been thrown into but suspected she wouldn't tell you even if she did. The race against the clock had only just begun and was already lost. By then, his body must be lying next to those of a dozen other anonymous people. From that point on, each minute would only bring about further decomposition of his body, in the earth and in your mind. You tried to summon a mental portrait of his face. You had no photograph. That image would have to be preserved at all costs. Though you had been with him just days before, you found yourself unable to now recall with any certainty his graceful features. His voice – could you even remember it? If you were having doubts after mere hours, how long until all of it – the dimple that deepened when you made him laugh, the smell of his hair, the promise to look after him that you had made his mother – was forever lost?

The smells of Cairo's streets clung to your nostrils, made you light-headed, caught in your throat. You took a few steps out of the traffic and into an unfamiliar alleyway. With your back leaning against a building, your body gave way without being ordered to do so. Then, only then, you placed your right hand over your eyes. Your fingers could not hold back the stream of tears.

24

Weeks passed, each one a slightly bleaker and more idle simulacrum of the last. The clinic had been cleaned, repaired, and put back in order. Walls repainted, supplies ordered – hypodermic needles, syringes, suture threads, gauze, vials, compresses – everything needed to stitch, treat, dress, and heal a wound. The damage caused by the ransacking of your clinic a month and a half earlier turned out to be mostly cosmetic. All that remained was a broken window-pane, whose replacement had been promised weeks ago. Tomorrow, inshallah. At first you'd made regular calls for someone to come fix it, but after a time you stopped bothering. The broken glass didn't block out the light. It merely stood as a reminder of what had happened, a witness to the fury of men. As time passed, it ceased to affect you at all, like the tufts of Tarboosh's fur you still sometimes found under the furniture and tossed in the garbage.

Without an assistant, you were performing fewer consultations at your Dokki practice. Sometimes half a day went by without a single patient. You could have closed up for a few hours and gone upstairs to see Mira, but you didn't. If anything, you were spending longer and longer hours on the first floor. You went up to your apartment only when it was dark enough outside for the broken window to go unnoticed.

Otherwise, your work was split between your weekly neurosurgery rotation at the American Hospital and your regular hours in Mokattam. Certain duties were fulfilled out of necessity, others out of habit. Sometimes you didn't open the Mokattam clinic at all.

The first time it happened, two hours went by before the locals went home, resigned and disconcerted by this uncharacteristic absence. You realized they were worried about you the next day, when you recognized a few zabbaleen children walking by your home, too far from their usual stomping grounds for mere coincidence. No doubt their parents had sent them to make sure nothing had happened to you. Not even the paradox of your patients worrying about their doctor's health brought a smile to your face. In the days that followed, you learned that an Islamic clinic was being built in Mokattam, just a few dozen metres from yours. Truth be told, your entire life had begun to seem futile.

All dialogue with your mother had broken down since your fight, and Nesrine gave up trying to mediate between you. Curiously, you found a certain peace in this new silence. With Mira, a completely new chasm had opened up. She had stopped leaving town, sensing that her homecomings would no longer work their fleeting magic. The contents of your pantry and bottles of bleach kept emptying out at a staggering pace, and you took pains to avert your eye. This cowardly, guilty failure could not be sustained forever. Each passing day drew you toward the discussion from which you shied away; in the end, Mira would find the courage you lacked.

At times like these, what is said matters little. It's everything else that counts. Mira gently tried to break your silence. You were surprised: no scenes, no outbursts. She seemed to weigh each word, describing her feelings as best she could while taking care not to lay all the blame on you. At times, her emotions got the better of her, and she would stop talking, rub away her tears, then take a deep breath and begin again. Her pain was sincere; you could imagine its intensity and understand its cause. Strangely, you were less moved by her pain than by her desire to spare you. She wasn't looking for someone to blame, just a way forward. She still loved you.

What did you have to offer her in return? No real apology or explanation. A collection of monosyllables, *I don't know*s and *What can I say*s. You had long ago relinquished your duties as a husband. She wanted to know where you stood – as if the two of you were plotting geographical coordinates. Did *you* even know where you stood? Were there even answers to these questions? You observed her pain without trying to meet it halfway; your suffering and hers had grown so far apart they would never again meet. She didn't mention Ali's name, perhaps hoping you might broach the subject. The subject was never broached.

Humankind is a nomadic species that has stopped moving. We are perfectly capable of going through life hiding from this fundamental truth; we convince ourselves that time doesn't count, space breaks down into dust, and this dust can be acquired with property and title. Orphaned from the vastness of life, we die without having lived. But the moment we come face to face with this truth, when it trains its harsh light on our daily lives, any compromise of our freedom becomes intolerable.

With the downcast eyes of someone beating a retreat, you mentioned Montreal for the first time. You had already looked into the formalities of emigrating to Canada. You'd be gone by the end of the month.

Now Mira saw clearly. All those weeks she'd spent trying to understand you, you had been plotting your escape. As you described your plans, Mira bristled. Her disbelief froze over into a mask of icy hate. You had often tried to guess at her reaction, but its intensity stopped you short. Then, a new thought, like an augury, yanked you from the numbness you had been floating in for months:

the fear that she might turn this violence inward. Mira, Mira, tragic heroine. The thought both terrified you and conjured up a cruelly vivid image of yourself as the architect of not just his own misfortune but also the ruin of everyone he ever loved.

And then, out of nowhere, came that reprehensible phrase, those words devoid of honour, that question whose sole possible answer was to bring into being this newborn vision of desolation.

'Do you want to come?'

Mira's mouth curled with contempt. She stared at you, and you felt her boiling wrath, long dormant like Armenia's volcanoes.

'Come for what? To be with who? A stranger?'

❦

Such is life: in a single action we can show courage toward ourselves and cowardice toward our loved ones. You set off on Christmas Eve, a holiday the women in your family would not celebrate that year. Fatheya wouldn't be asked to make her shushbarak for New Year's Day, when you would all keep eating dumplings until someone found the King Farouk coin your mother had hidden in one. In the months ahead, parliamentary elections would be held. The president swore they would be free and fair. What did you care about promises made to a country you were leaving?

You left as one sets off for a long time, as one sheds a language that will cease to be spoken or a nickname that will not be used again. You tried not to attach undue importance to what remained, after all, a series of details. Slamming a door without knowing whether you would ever push it open again; eating a dish with no certainty that you would taste it again; an incomplete – *inevitably* incomplete – list of people not told you were leaving … You went to gather up a handful of photos, hoping they might one day make you feel more joy than shame.

One photograph shows you and your parents, at a time when life had yet to reveal its full store of adversity. In another, Nesrine's face is caught between adolescence and adulthood. And there is one of you as well, standing in front of the Mokattam clinic that was your pride and joy. You, standing pensively before Mira in her wedding dress, wearing her wedding smile. You didn't have any of Fatheya – what occasion was there for a photograph of you with the maid? And of course there were none of Ali. Eventually, you placed them all back in the family album you'd pulled them from and put it back on the shelf it never should have left.

When you said goodbye to your mother, she answered with a shake of her head that could have meant a thousand things: *My son, when will I see you again? See where your stubbornness has led you! Have you ever even asked yourself what will become of us without you?* Perhaps it meant none of the above, perhaps all. You took Nesrine in your arms, without saying a thing, as if words were not bound to answer to tears. You'd heard that Mira had gone to stay with her parents for a few days, and you hadn't bothered to find out if it was true. You never finished the letter you'd started to write to her; what use is it to try to explain something you don't understand yourself? By breaking your vows, as if they were your sole property, you abandoned her to her insoluble regrets. For years she would wonder what she might have been, what she might have done so that you wouldn't have stopped loving her.

As you turned to close the door, you saw a silhouette coming toward you.

'What about me? Aren't you going to say goodbye?'

Shame sent the blood rushing to your cheeks, which had hollowed out in the last few weeks. You made a move toward her, but Fatheya waved you sharply away. Her voice was choked up, her inflections unfamiliar.

'Were you really going to leave like a thief in the night? Which one of us taught you to run out on your loved ones like that? Who?'

'Sorry, Faty, I'm exhausted ... '

She softened, came over to you, and hugged your body, drained of all resistance. She spoke to you as if you were still the child you wished you had never stopped being.

'Tarek, I'm not sure you really have it in you, but try to take care of yourself, okay?'

'You, too ... and take care of them.'

With arms accustomed to thankless work, she squeezed you vigorously, until she felt an upwelling of emotion. Then she made that impatient shooing movement usually reserved for the flies buzzing around her pots and pans. It was time to go.

Home, cab, airport, plane, airport, cab ... Snow covered the streets of this unknown city in a dirty grey blanket that would soon be familiar to you. From that day on, you would be everywhere a stranger.

25

'You didn't need to come.'

'Why, aren't you happy to see me?'

'Yes, of course … I just mean, you shouldn't have been worried.'

'Because you have to be worried to visit your brother?'

'No, no, of course not … '

Nesrine said nothing. Her silences were a stretched canvas onto which the past projected images. You hadn't seen her in four years, a number that took some reckoning to arrive at. Since landing in this new country, your sense of time had become less precise. At first, you had to carefully tally each month spent in this unfamiliar place and report it to multiple levels of government as part of your immigration process. Then, as your papers came through, your obsession with the number of months faded. The Quebecers you worked with all carried detailed memories of the last five or six winters and could recall the finer points of each. There was the one when the snow didn't finally stick until Christmas, the one when the road salt was no match for the freezing rain, the one when, in their expert opinion, the big wet snowflakes were still falling in April. But you had lost count. No city changes more with the seasons than Montreal. You were insensitive even to that.

You had been forced to start your medical career all over again, at the bottom. With an unrecognized Egyptian medical degree, you could not practise as a doctor. You thought about becoming a nurse.

Even though you were overqualified, the union wouldn't let you work without a nursing diploma. For want of anything better to do, you settled on a job as a nurse's aide, a position not governed by a professional order. You held that job for six months before obtaining an equivalency. Since your internship in Cairo was also not recognized, you had to do another one in your new country. Your high evaluations qualified you for surgery, your specialty. A year later, you began a residency at the university hospital.

You unfurled this long story for Nesrine, who'd simply asked how you liked your job. When you saw that you were losing her in a flurry of details that meant nothing to her, you cut your story short. *Yes. The people are nice.* Her subtle nod made her curls of black hair quiver.

You were reminded of a man in Mokattam whom you'd treated for a pneumopathy. The way every breath was a battle for him. There was a time when talking to Nesrine had come to you as naturally as breathing. But just like that man's belaboured breathing, it now felt as if you had to carefully weigh each word. Mokattam was several thousand miles away and so, too, at that moment, was your sister. She burrowed under a colourless flannel blanket on your sofa.

Heavy minutes dragged by. You finally broke the silence.

'Shall we play?'

Nesrine made a sudden movement that belied her body's numbness.

'Play what?'

'You know what,' you said in a gentle voice. 'Come on. Your guess.'

When she exhaled, her nostrils twitched.

'Is it a woman?'

'No, not a woman.'

'A fictional character?'

'No.'

'A relative?'

'No.'

She raised her eyes skyward, as if to deny that she was getting caught up in the game.

'A politician?'

'No, not a politician.'

'Singer, actor … ?'

'No … '

'Egyptian?'

You nodded.

'Ah, well! Is he on TV?'

'No.'

'A family friend?'

'No.'

'C'mon. If he's not famous, and he's not part of the family, and he's not one of our friends, how can you … '

She paused, then resumed in a disenchanted voice:

'Dead?'

You nodded, and watched the light drain from her eyes.

'Tarek, why bring this up?'

'I can only answer yes or no until you say his name.'

'Very well,' she said with a new hardness. 'Did this person destroy our family?'

'Nesrine … '

'Oh right, my bad. It was you who destroyed our family. He should have just stayed in his garbage dump.'

'Don't … '

'*Yes* or *no*, Tarek. You're the one who wanted to play.'

She seemed surprised by the sound of her own voice, like someone who catches fright at the sight of their shadow in a dimly lit alley. She pulled herself together.

'Do you regret meeting him?'

'I don't know, I just … '

'Yes or no, Tarek?'

'No … '

'Do you know how much you've hurt us?'

'What about me? Do you really think I didn't hurt myself? That I didn't want to die?'

She seemed to hesitate before asking her last question.

'Did you love him?'

Your voice was tied in knots. You knew that the slightest extra syllable would burst the dam holding back your emotion.

'Did you love him?'

🕊

Once the bandage was ripped off, the scarring process could begin. Nesrine told you about her wedding, which you hadn't attended, and her son, whose photos you were seeing for the first time. You knew your absence had hurt her. You tried to make up for lost time by asking about her life. You pretended to be moved by her tales of life as a young mother, to be eager to meet the man she was making her life with. It wasn't her stories themselves that were important to you, but the simple act of being with your sister again, how her familiar voice cut through the cloud of worry that hung over your life. What was said ultimately mattered little.

A note of reproach sometimes crept into your sister's stories. You pretended not to notice. You could well imagine how lonely your mother must have been, in a family home that had grown far too large. Your departure an affront that she never recovered from. Though it was not enough to make you feel guilt, you knew that your absence still hung over the walls of the Dokki villa. You began to wonder whether Nesrine married as a way out, just as you chose exile in Quebec. She had wed at thirty-five, late in Egypt in the

1980s. You couldn't say to what extent her choice had been shaped by love or fear, exhaustion or calculation. You secretly wondered if having a family might have been her way to give your mother something of the future she'd imagined for herself. As Nesrine's story unfolded, you realized for the first time that the attention lavished on you by your parents, their way of focusing their ambitions on you to the near total exclusion of others, had caused Nesrine suffering. All these years, you'd never imagined that your sister might be jealous of something you experienced only as a burden.

Little by little, you began to let your sister into your life. With no clear sense of where to start, you told her about the flooding in Montreal the year before. Storm drains overflowing, vehicles caught in the water, the Décarie Expressway a swimming pool ... As your sister's sole experience of snow was the mountains of Lebanon, where you'd travelled with your parents, you tried to describe the Quebec winter. You told her about this province with dreams of being a country. To make her laugh, you even tried to imitate the Quebec accent, such a far cry from the one you and she had grown up with. That, at long last, coaxed a smile from her.

Nesrine was surprised you hadn't connected with the hundreds of Egyptian Levantine families that had also settled in Montreal. Did you have any friends here? You nodded, evasively. A special someone in your life? She didn't dare ask. After a while you brought up the association that supported people living with Huntington's disease. You volunteered with them. She didn't know exactly why you'd chosen this cause but could tell it was close to your heart. You had talked about everything else, and now you were at last revealing something of yourself. It wasn't much, but it touched her all the same.

❦

On Sunday mornings you went running. Nesrine hadn't heard you come in, and you didn't want to interrupt her conversation. She only realized you were there when she was about to hang up. She started; you smiled. Not knowing how long you'd been there, she took the lead.

'It was Maman.'

'Is she well?'

'Yes. She sends her love.'

You were about to say something like *I see she found my phone number*, but stopped yourself. The silence between you was as much your fault as your mother's, and it wasn't Nesrine's role to apportion blame. A calm had descended over the last few days, and you were determined to maintain the truce. You went to take a shower.

The next hour passed in near silence. After a while, Nesrine announced that she was cutting short her stay.

'Weren't you supposed to leave in a week?'

'No, today.'

'Is it something I did?'

'No, don't be silly.'

'It's good to see you, you know?'

'For me, too, Tarek … for me, too.'

You'd learned to pretend not to notice when your sister was about to cry. You took her in your arms, an old instinct. Her fingers dug into the small of your back, as if clinging to the moment. You saw the two of you again, on the beach at Montaza. There was a game you used to play to see who could hold sea water in their palms the longest. Your hands were bigger, but you sometimes spread your fingers to let her win. The game would last only a few seconds.

'What time's your flight? We might have time for brunch, I know a great place. Not as good as Fatheya's beans, but good omelettes … '

'That's nice of you, but my cab should be here any minute.'

'There's no way to change your mind?'

She didn't answer. Your smile had fully deserted you. She left you to your silence, and you contemplated the breadth of the chasm between you. It would take more to bridge it than the fluorescent lights of a North American diner, more than the memory of the haphazardly spiced beans of your childhood. The same past that brought you together kept you apart.

Your right hand freed hers from the handle of her suitcase. You calmly escorted her to the front door of your building. Once it opened, the sound of the city injected a touch of life to your last moments together. Leaning against the wall, she looked distractedly out at the traffic.

'What is it you remember?'

You didn't see what she meant.

'Je me souviens. On the licence plates.'

'Oh, right. That's Quebec's motto. I asked a colleague what it meant once. He just shrugged. I don't think anyone here even remembers what they're supposed to remember. Maybe that's for the best in the end.'

'Maybe.'

The cab had just pulled up. She kissed you as the driver placed her luggage in the trunk. She had something to say and had waited for the last possible moment.

'You never asked how Mira was … '

'Has something happened to her?'

You felt stupid. You couldn't tell whether you'd been trying to avoid the subject or hoping that Nesrine would bring it up. *Mira.* That name alone had the power to dredge up the guilty conscience you'd been holding beneath the surface for years. That name knew of your loves and your cowardice, your regrets and your selfishness. The words you didn't say before leaving, the actions that might have brought comfort. *Has something happened to her?* How stupid:

you knew all too well what had happened to her, and whose fault it was. Nesrine had gotten into the back of the car. Absorbed in your thoughts, you didn't see her wave goodbye. You were sure that she was leaving before she got the chance to tell you why she had come.

26

Cairo, 1999

Cumin, dust (already), coriander, benzine, donkeys and their excrement, sand, dust (again), sweat, cardamom, burning fuel, fried onions, burnt garbage, hot beans, jasmine, dust (ever and always), asphalt growing soft under the unchecked reign of the sun ... The constituents of Cairo's heady olfactory aura go unnoticed until the day we leave the city and return to encounter them afresh. Before that, they are simply not there: abstract like our heartbeats, vital but imperceptible. They come to exist only once you've lived without them, returning with a violent clarity, their presence invasive where once it was anodyne. For you, at that moment, these smells *were* Cairo.

Vertigo swept over you as you walked down the airstairs to the tarmac at Cairo International. After just a few steps, you felt your legs give way. You clung to the handrail as the passenger in front of you barely caught your suitcase. The sky was stained ochre by the khamaseen, the landscape sepia-toned like an old postcard. Each of the moments you were soon to experience was already in the process of becoming a faded memory. Indifferent to your thoughts, the wind kept on sweeping its burning sand from one desert to another. You looked no further to explain your suddenly moist eyes and belaboured breathing.

The same first and last name, but no one around who can pronounce them without massacring them: that, too, is exile. The same first and last name, but that was more or less all you had in common with the man you used to be.

Fifteen years had passed since you set foot on the dusty soil of your homeland. Fifteen years spent methodically forgetting the white flesh of the melons of Ismailia, the parking lot of the Palace Cinema, where images of American films played out on the distant screen, the Fairouz and Édith Piaf tapes your mother played during meals, the horse-drawn carriages along Alexandria's Corniche promenade, the taste of the year's first sea urchins on Agami Beach, and so much more.

You were fifty years old, and somewhere deep inside you knew this would be the last time you'd return.

Your mother had died three days earlier. The sound of Nesrine's broken voice on the phone affected you, perhaps more than the news itself. The truth was that you had felt like an orphan for years. You'd turned down your sister's invitation to stay with her. Disappointed, she'd tried to convince you: she would introduce you to her son, who'd be so happy to meet his uncle. You pictured yourself at his age, forced to answer the monotonous questions of the countless adults who, in those loosely defined Middle Eastern 'families,' were all introduced as aunts and uncles. Under your parents' watchful eye, you would give the same answers: you had lots of friends, good grades in math, and wanted to be a doctor (*like your father*, they would hasten to add if you forgot to mention it unprompted). Who could ever believe that a twelve-year-old would happily make conversation with an adult who was a complete stranger? You didn't bring it up again; she didn't insist.

As you'd made your sister promise, no one came to pick you up at the airport. In English, you asked the cab driver to take you to your childhood villa, though no one in your family lived there anymore. Mistaking you for a foreigner, he devised an ingeniously circuitous route to the neighbourhood where you'd spent most of your life. It didn't matter. For that evening you were just another tourist. No one was waiting for you. From time to time, the driver tried to start a conversation in a patchwork of English and Arabic. You answered with polite shakes of your head, pretended not to understand when he addressed you in a language that was no longer your own. As you passed the Groppi tea room on Soliman Pasha Square, he tried again.

'Hena Groppi. Very good place, look!'

With the knuckle of his index finger, he rapped on his car window, and you pretended to see the patisserie's Haussmann-style facade for the first time. How could he know how many ice creams you and Nesrine had eaten there as children? There was the Joséphine Baker, the Trois petits cochons, and the Boule-de-neige that Nesrine ordered without fail. The checkered marble floor, the staircase leading to the reception hall, the clinking of silver cutlery… As you drifted in and out of your reverie, he realized he would not get a single word out of you. He switched on his radio with a sharp, resigned click. A droning voice came on. You ignored it.

The funeral would be held the next day. You were sure to meet Nesrine's husband there. What did he know of the reasons for your departure? In what words would your sister have couched the story? Or had he already known, before she told him? Did your name come up at Sunday dinners, dished up along with second helpings of Fatheya's mulukhiyah? And what of the family friends, the ones you had grown up with, who had been cared for first by your father and in turn by you? All of Cairo would be there, or rather all of *Egypt*, since Cairenes never pronounce the name of their capital, preferring to call their city state *Egypt*, with all its epic associations.

What would they really think when they first saw you again? What would their eyes reveal? And would you really manage to ignore their reactions, as you had convinced yourself when you bought your plane ticket?

27

The space that had been your father's clinic before it became your own was now a clothing store. You checked out the Western-style dresses and suits in the store window. They were selling vulgar coverings for the bodies you had learned to care for. After staring for a few moments at the expressionless mannequins crowded into the window, you turned away.

In time, the central staircase had become hard for your mother to climb. She had relented and agreed to move into a 1930s-style building with an elevator. But she was loath to move down in the world and refused to give up the family villa in Dokki. The main floor had become a retail space, and the second and third floors had been converted into four rental apartments, two per level. Just one, on the second floor, stood vacant. Unable to fully relinquish the building, your mother had held on to one of the apartments, 'for visitors.' In truth, no one had ever slept there before you.

Nesrine hadn't told you that she wanted to be there with you, to open the door to those last few square metres over which your mother would no longer reign. And that meant you never got the chance to tell her that you'd rather be alone. In fact, you hadn't told each other anything important. She'd been content to leave the key with the doorman.

You unlocked the front door haltingly, like a tourist surprised that March in Cairo isn't cooler. I wish I could have read the expression on your face with some semblance of certainty. I'd have liked to be able to study the composition of emotions – fatigue, nostalgia, sadness, eagerness, renunciation, and indifference – that inhabited your movements. Before I had time, you became a shadow awkwardly following another, the doorman's, before disappearing inside the weathered building.

Four years had passed since she moved to the new apartment, yet you could have sworn that her scent still suffused this one. She had never been willing to change her fragrance. Years earlier, when Caron stopped producing her Infini, she had, God only knows how, secured a supply that lasted till the very end. Infini: how apt for a woman who rejected all limitations. You threw open the blinds, and the outside air rushed in, an invading army breaching the defences of a dying empire.

The apartment felt bigger than the one you had in Montreal. You could scarcely believe it was just half of the floor your sister and mother had once shared, above the one where you and Mira lived. You sat on the sofa with your back to the window. From outside, it was objectively impossible to see your hand caressing the seat, as if seeking out some remnant of human warmth that death had so far neglected to ferry over – yet I'm certain I saw it. With eyes closed, I imagined you making your way through the rooms, trying to conjure the memory of each place as you had known it then. Here, a hallway had been narrowed to accommodate a bathroom; there, a new bedroom took up just half the space of the former master bedroom.

Never had I been so physically close to what I had always imagined; in fact, I was almost right there. You pushed open the door; the room was tidy. Who had last made the bed? Fatheya, surely. Your gaze tired of trying to track every knick-knack and figure out every change that these last fifteen years had brought. A shiver of guilt crept up your neck, then down your spine. As a child, your parents' bedroom had been off limits when they weren't home. You took a few steps toward a kitchen that had not existed then. Everything was neatly arranged, save for a pile of letters on the table.

Your name was written on each envelope, in the same handwriting. The top left-hand corner contained the sender's contact details. And his name. Ali.

You sat down gingerly, as if the room were mined with explosives set to trip at the slightest false movement. Your father's pocket watch sat on top of the pile of envelopes to keep them from flying away. Next to it, a bowl of umm Ali. Whoever had laid this table knew exactly what they were doing. By placing everything just so, *I* had known what *I* was doing. My heart was like a bird flailing around against the walls of my rib cage, unable to bear another second of captivity. And I know it was the same for yours. At that moment both were beating to the same frantic, irregular rhythm. We each had our own reasons.

The letters were stacked in chronological order, with the oldest on top. The space for the destination address was blank. A date had been written in by another hand. *March 1991*. Seven years after Ali's death. Seven years after you left for Montreal. The most recent had clearly been mailed. It was postmarked *October 1995*.

You felt suddenly spied upon, struck by the premonition that the author of this *mise en scène* might be in the apartment. Your chair legs made the floorboards creak. You leapt up and set off in search of a potential intruder, possibly lying in wait since you got there. As you entered your mother's bedroom, you walked not like the child who had trodden so lightly to avoid detection but like a wild beast in search of hidden prey. Your hands yanked open closet doors. Surprised garments puffed up with air, hangers squealed on their rods. Metal on metal. Everything seemed suspect. You thrust a key noisily into the lock of a large empty safe. Metal on metal. The door handle yielded to your blows. Metal. You finally convinced yourself you were alone in the apartment. Alone with those letters. This was not the place to read them. You stuffed them in an envelope of unimportant things, because nothing mattered anymore. Thick notes of Infini still clung in the air. Metallic.

You warily closed the apartment door. Your movements were nervous, you felt vulnerable with your back to the hallway. A neighbour opened her second-floor door. You jumped. I stood there, waiting for you to leave the building.

Here's how it was supposed to go. I'd pretend to be there by chance. Walk up to you and ask directions. An address you'd still remember? I'd decided it should be, so you could stop, picture the route, and then start giving me directions. But it must not look suspicious either. No, above all, that. Not an address that meant something to you. That was the trick: an address of no significance, but one you could place. I'd steal the moment you'd take to consider the best route. I'd steal a look, a few words, the smell of your breath. These would be as precious to me as the letters I'd parted with would be to you. A fair trade. Would you wonder, when you saw me, if something was going on? Would you have some kind of premonition? An instinct? Then, somewhere in the depths of your incredulous gaze, I'd have the courage to invite you for a drink in some quiet place where we could talk. I'd tell you everything. Everything I knew. Everything I had imagined. I'd tell you all about your absence; I'd tell you how long I'd been waiting. And you'd tell me why. It would be like being born again, but with you present this time. I would make my way properly into the world. But the last thing I needed was to start crying before I had the chance to tell you everything. Not before I had the chance to call you *Father*. Not before I heard you say *son*.

I saw you in the doorway. You stepped out. I walked over to ask directions. Words went racing through my mind; they wanted to reach you, but none came out. You pushed me violently away. You were almost running. You didn't look back. Then you were gone. Aware that I'd just missed my first chance to talk to you, I let this body collapse, this body that had failed to utter a single sentence while there was still time. I wanted to dissolve into my own powerlessness.

ME

28

Cairo, 1996

Every letter had been opened: the oldest by your mother, my grand-mother Mémie; the most recent by me, who discovered the pile in the drawer. I had read and reread them until I could recite them by heart. The fact that I didn't always understand what they said was enough to make them unforgettable.

When Mémie had to move, we'd gone with her. It had taken time, but we'd eventually found an apartment that met her needs: a single floor in a building with an elevator. My mother and I lived in the right wing, which had a guest room where Aunt Nesrine sometimes stayed; Mémie was on the opposite side. The two wings converged on the central rooms: living room, kitchen, sitting room, dining room, and powder room. The furniture we'd brought with us from Dokki felt too big, even in such a spacious apartment. Only someone who had known the villa could understand why we had such a massive chandelier hanging in the dining room of an apartment with such a low ceiling. Our dishes would often brush up against the crystal pendants with a tinkling that exasperated Mémie.

When my grandmother was out, I liked to spend time in her apartment. I'd lean against the outside wall of her room, reading a book and waiting for her to find me there. I had no reason to be there. But it wasn't expressly forbidden, which was enough for me.

I wasn't yet twelve the first time I went through her drawers. They were normally locked, but on that day the key was left in the keyhole. A carelessness most unlike my grandmother. That was when I found the letters. I don't remember the exact date, but it must have matched the date on the last letter. I held on to that key. I was afraid Mémie would find out, but she never said anything to me. Truth be told, I didn't feel especially guilty. I was well aware that I shouldn't be seen, that being discovered there, reading those letters, could only work against me – but I didn't feel like I was doing anything wrong, exactly. Whoever caught me would be more embarrassed than I was. In a sense, those letters belonged to me: Weren't they the best way I'd found to fill in the gaps left by your unsayable absence?

Only later did I wonder whether they hadn't known all along of my secret reading in my grandmother's bedroom. What sort of fool's bargain had drawn them together, unbeknownst to me? Perhaps my trespass came as a distraction in that stifling theatre where the same dramas played out day after day, acts of a single play where nothing happened though the performance stretched out over a lifetime. On the cusp of old age, the actresses were still onstage, reciting their lines and losing themselves in a series of pointless adventures that never resolved into a unified plot.

Mémie was a warrior, tragédienne par excellence. Her daughter had nicknamed her Napoléone, as much for her strict rule as her nervous, defensive bearing. She might have gone down in history as a protagonist of epic dramas, responsible for glorious conquests and broken pacts with devils, popes, and emperors, had fate seen fit to grant the station to which her character predestined her. Not born an empress, she had to satisfy herself by exerting power on the small scale of her immediate environment. By casting her in the role it had done, History had shown itself cruelly lacking in vision.

Nesrine, her daughter, your sister, my aunt, fated to be ever stuck in secondary roles. She had the foresight to leave home and get married – as if there were any other way for an Egyptian woman between the two millennia to leave home – and have a child, to search out the oxygen and light that were growing scarcer in her family home and even have some in reserve to share with me on her visits. She had always known how to fulfill what little was expected of her. Her quick wit and mischievous smile never deserted her.

There was my mother. Mira, Mira, fading flower: the first become last, she who had stumbled into resignation without anyone knowing how or why. She was possessed of a wary sweetness, an expression dulled by the fear of showing the lines disappointment had traced on her face. She whose soul had been drained of all joy, like a dish-cloth wrung out after use. The one we pitied, who didn't deserve what life gave her – as if happiness had ever been meted out based on merit, through some kind of double-entry bookkeeping that rewards one in proportion to the other.

Fatheya: assigned the role of standing ever in the wings, delivering prompts. She was the one we paid, and this transactional relationship seems to sum up nearly everything. She was the one there to *do things* (two words that raised Mémie's ire in my school compositions, both cursed with a sense so broad they ceased to mean anything at all). She *did* the housework, cooking, washing, and shopping, while bowing before her employer and offering tea to guests. She *did* the carpets, and the crystal, all the while making as little noise as possible.

The tragedy being played out in this room hinged on the fact that its hero – you – never appeared.

My role was to stand in as a reminder of your absence, a measure of the passage of time. I was their light, their sense of wonder. Often subject of conversations, occasional object of concern. I was an extension of them, some form of second chance, the glue that bonded them, the reason to gather and the pretext to call. Their guilt, their giving up, their petty cowardice. I was their guilty conscience. And though they never said as much, I somehow always knew I was like you.

I didn't understand those letters, but I loved them. Those letters spoke you. Though I had no way of knowing it yet, they were at once shameful and sublime, written in the halting Arabic of someone who had learned to write late in life. They plodded along, shaky in syntax but alive with the breath of toil, doubt, and sweat. Every word on each page carried in it the fear of being ridiculous, of getting lost or intercepted, of never reaching you. Redolent of cheap paper, of crossing out, and lack. They never said 'I love you,' but each one said *I love you*. They never came out and said what they meant, and at that age I was too young to read between the lines.

Each letter began like this: 'Tarek, I hope this finds you well. Your mother told me she told you everything, God bless her. She told me you were happy and that you understood.' Or: 'Tarek, I hear you're a great doctor over there. I understand that you don't have time to answer me. I hope you don't resent me.' One contained a phrase that stood out from the rest: 'Do you still believe in entangled photons?' Each ended with the same three letters:

علي. Ali.

That April afternoon, I was sitting on the floor of Mémie's room. A few weeks had passed since I'd gotten my hands on the correspondence. I must have been eleven. The rectangular window frame projected onto the floor a distorted patch of light, its contours freed from their original right angles. I loved that light. With arms outstretched, I pored over the pages of the letters. Betrayed by their cheap paper, they turned transparent in the light, their backward lines bleeding through from the other side. Page after page, I discovered the uneven spacing between words and irregular trace of a handwriting that gets tighter as the available space shrinks. I found the worn-out lines of the most recent letters. The ones in which even the handwriting expressed the abdication of any hope of an answer. Cruel light. I was trying to figure out the words written on the back of a page when Fatheya's muffled voice emerged.

'Rafik, hurry up! Mémie's coming!'

I quickly stuffed the letters into envelopes, folding sheets of paper back over themselves, creases be damned, slammed the drawer shut, and distanced myself from the dresser full of stories.

'What are you doing here?'

I didn't answer. There was no denying that I was in fact *here*. Undeniably *here*, guiltily *here*. Anything I said would be used against me. Mémie looked at me from her bedside perch, like the improbable pigeon towers on Egyptian roadsides. She scanned my face. My face revealed nothing. She inspected my hands. My hands were empty. I felt an apprehension cross her mind. A sudden intuition. She again scanned my face and hands. Her nostrils twitched with a suspicious sniff. She went to her dressing table, opened the bottles, moved the nail polishes, unscrewed the lipsticks. Everything was in place. She seemed to have found her composure, if not the thing she was looking for. Her breathing slowed to normal. She shook her head at me. The sentence had been handed down, and it was unexpectedly lenient. I left.

As it happened, Mémie had other fish to fry. Jacques Chirac had chosen Lebanon and Egypt for his first state visit to the Middle

East. As she was Lebanese by birth, Egyptian by residency, and above all French through cultural transubstantiation, these current events had fully mobilized her attention. A few weeks earlier, she'd made a trip to the nearby barracks, where the military band was floundering through the 'Marseillaise,' to give them pistachio biscuits and implore them to perform the French anthem with the reverence it deserved. Suffice to say, it would take more than my incursion into her room to dampen her high spirits.

After kicking me out, she finished making herself up and then sank into the living room armchair where, in a state of exaltation, she would listen three times to the French leader's address. This was the fifth and final day on which his regional tour had been broadcast, and she did not intend to miss a single word. Annoyed by the voice of the interpreter speaking the president's words into Arabic, she was straining to make out each phrase in its original language.

Il est des pays qui, plus que d'autres, nous parlent, nous attirent, nous inspirent. Des pays dont l'histoire, le génie, le patrimoine suscitent en nous le rêve, l'admiration et l'émotion. Parmi ces pays, l'Égypte vient au premier rang …

'Et la France!' she cheered in her living room, as if returning a personal compliment.

'Et la France! Et la France!' Fatheya repeated, phonetically, mimicking her employer's patriotically outstretched index finger. She looked at me, certain of the effect she was having, then patted me on the back of the head. It was her way of absolving me.

'And be more careful next time!'

These warnings and reproaches always betrayed the same tender concern. Cryptic as it tended to be, *be careful* had been the main job assigned to me from a young age. Fatheya's admonitions applied to the full gamut of risks, from adults approaching me on the street to the chill in the air lurking in wait the second I left the confines of the family home. Come to think of it, though, this was the first time I had had to be careful *in* the house.

'I was reading letters from my father ... well, letters *to* my father. I say that, but I know you know.'

She started meticulously wiping down the surface of the fridge to avoid my question.

'How come we didn't send him the letters? Some were old. Years old, even. Doesn't Mémie know where he lives?'

The fridge had never been so clean, yet Fatheya's cloth continued its frenzied dance over its surface. I went on with my monologue.

'Who's Ali?'

The cloth hung motionless in the air.

'You're getting on my nerves!'

'You knew about the letters.'

'What can I say?'

'Do I look like my father?'

She seemed surprised.

'You're as stubborn as he was ... '

I would learn nothing further that day. I left the kitchen without a sound. My grandmother had her back to me, too busy drinking in the words of the Président de la République to notice my presence. Chirac was evoking the chimera of an Egypt with one foot in Europe, a better world waiting to be built. The new world he described bore an uncanny resemblance to yesterday's, the one Mémie had so cherished before it disappeared forever. His speech went on a few more minutes before she was forced to return to the reality of her own country, where the French language had been falling out of use as her community hollowed out. I left her to her illusions.

❧

What I know about you, I learned from Fatheya. We'd wait until the other women's duties took them from the apartment, and then I'd ask questions, sitting in the kitchen while she prepared the meal. I would go downstairs with my schoolbag and notebooks, my homework a ready excuse if we got caught. Mémie was suspicious of my spending time with the maid, but I reassured her with the argument that it was better for someone to keep an eye on her as she cooked. We all knew how Fatheya got carried away with the spices. It gave me a plausible excuse. What I know about you smelled of garlic and anise.

The stories poured out of Fatheya, as might be expected from a woman grown accustomed to not being listened to, who finds herself with an audience late in life. She'd say whatever popped into her head, teach me slang words, tell me about her despair the day Abdel Halim Hafez died ('Many women have thrown themselves off balconies, you know? For love, for country, religion … but only he could sing of all those things!'). She shared stratagems for chasing away the hens that wandered into the villa ('You could never imagine how they lose their feathers when they start to panic, those wild creatures!'). I'd have been hard-pressed to find a subject Fatheya didn't feel strongly about. Yet she rarely talked about herself. What type of man had she desired? Where were the children who had torn her earlobe tugging on her earrings? She didn't have one word to say on any of these matters. She far preferred to regale me with stories of Mémie's everyday meanness. Her fondness for this topic knew no bounds. She would kick off with an *I shouldn't be telling you this, but*, which provided the rhetorical cover to start in on her litany of recriminations against her employer. She knew I would never report her to my grandmother. I was the person she could vent to; she the one who held out a roundabout route to you. There was a give and a take. Always I tried to bring her back to the one subject I cared about, you, because I knew that once the surge began there was no stemming the flow of Fatheya's digressions. She spoke much as she cooked, with generous portions, if not always balanced flavours. She was at her best with dishes whose cooking time was unimportant. I listened patiently to her stories of hens in the hope that, sooner or later, you might play a role.

I didn't dare ask my family about you. I could see the effect it had: my mother's bitterness, Mémie's furrowed brow, Nesrine's embarrassment. I suspected that the mention of your name had once inspired only love and pride. What could you have done to bring about this change of heart? When I discovered the letters my grandmother had kept under lock and key, I was convinced they must hold at least part of the answer. I refrained from mentioning their existence, for fear of falling prey to the same disenchantment. To limit the risk of contagion, I decided to stick to what I had been told about you as a child.

That your name was Tarek.

That you were the eldest child.

That you were a doctor (like your father).

That you'd moved to Canada.

That everything was for the best that way.

Fatheya was the only one left from whom I could learn a little more about the father life had denied me. With an almost adolescent hand, I was painting a pointillist portrait, guided by Fatheya's scattered clues. She often repeated and sometimes contradicted herself, but would never admit it. And she always tailored her narrative to fit my mood. You were raised up above all others when she felt that was what I needed. You were selfish, and not altogether innocent, on days when I was strong enough to take it. As I drifted off to sleep, new questions bubbled up. I'd repeat them to myself, so as not to forget them, and then file them away in the same mental drawer as Ali's letters. Like your letters, these questions were left orphaned, unanswered. Fatheya never flat-out refused to answer my questions. She sometimes tried to dodge them, but her clumsy pirouettes were ineffective against an obstinate child like me. For a long time, I thought she took me into her confidence out of affection, but the more I thought about it, the clearer it became that telling me about you was a salve to her as well.

'But still … did he know about me, when he left?'

The one time I'd dared ask my mother that question, she was overtaken by an anger I hoped to never see again. Years later, I tried my luck once more, with Fatheya this time. I feigned detachment, tried to casually slip in my question among the others, like an onlooker in the winding streets of Khan al-Khalili. Fatheya shook her head.

'And does he know now?'

'No, Rafik.'

'Why doesn't someone tell him?'

'I don't know why. Your mother didn't want us to. We were forbidden from mentioning him in her presence. It was either that or never see you again. I thought Nesrine would tell him when she went to see him, but in the end she and your grandmother did what Mira wanted. Everyone figured he'd come back eventually, that your mother would tell him then. Well, I guess anyway. After all, it was nobody's business but hers. Do you understand?'

I didn't understand but nodded anyway. A silence. She didn't know what to say; I pondered the implications of her last words.

'Maybe it's all for the best in the end. It means he hasn't abandoned me. You can't abandon someone who doesn't exist.'

'Oh, yes! He's abandoned quite enough people as it is! Your mother, Mémie … everyone who counted on him.'

'Do you think he'd have left if he'd known about me?'

'You sure ask a lot of questions … How should I know? I think he left because he didn't really have a choice. Things were getting complicated.'

'Was it because of Ali?'

Every crease and wrinkle on Fatheya's face emphasized the words of warning that followed.

'Do not *ever* say that name in front of Mémie! Or anyone else, for that matter. You'll get yourself into trouble, and me, too!'

'So it *is* because of Ali?"

'Yes, yes. You're right about that … '

'But you still won't tell me who he is?'

29

Only after I began writing to you did that memory come back to me. There must always be some explanation for all the details, the seemingly minor ones that we somehow forget to forget. We were on our way to Montaza Beach. Mémie claimed Alexandria was the only place in Egypt whose air was bearable in summer. She was scheduled to arrive a couple days before us, with Nesrine and her husband and child, to get the apartment ready. I'm not sure what this entailed, or why Fatheya couldn't have done it, but the arrangement seemed to suit everyone.

We set off early, eating in the car while my mother drove. The start of that vacation tasted of La Vache qui rit spread on pita bread, lazily sprinkled with za'atar to suggest a meal had been prepared. Every time we stopped for gas, I was allowed to choose a treat: a tacit contract designed to keep me on my best behaviour. Fatheya took me to the store while my mother filled the tank. The vanilla wafers came wrapped in pairs, six to a pack. Even so, they were cheaper than the imported Western chocolate bars, sold individually. That was enough to convince Fatheya to choose them for me; nothing could challenge the argument that we were *getting our money's worth*. Oily puddles with iridescent streaks in metallic hues smeared the parking lot. Fatheya claimed they might burst into flames at any moment in this heat, starting a fire that would blow the gas station to smithereens. She'd seen it on TV. I took great pains not to let the puddles come in contact with my sandals. I hopped around, in a miasma of gas fumes, like someone dancing atop an erupting volcano. I wiped the wafer crumbs stuck to my upper lip with the back of my hand. Fatheya praised the choice of sweets to my mother, giving me the credit. We had gotten our money's worth. I was six years old.

We had just arrived and were heading to the apartment to drop off our suitcases. Fatheya was recovering her human form after the walk of a few dozen metres that threatened to liquefy her. We let her take a shower and finish tidying up before joining us at the beach. Nesrine and Mémie were lying on deck chairs set up on the small concrete slab where our cabin stood. What we called a *cabin* was in fact a small white bungalow with a kitchen, washroom, and storage spaces, separated from the others by a green trellis fence. I remember that we were not to touch that fence, which might give us a splinter. I wanted to run to my aunt and surprise her by putting my hands on her shoulders, but I let out an excited yelp that betrayed my presence and startled only myself. Nesrine and Mémie turned around. I left my beach bag at my mother's feet and rushed toward them.

I don't remember when exactly these events were set in motion. I'd gone swimming with Nesrine first, and the salty taste of swallowed sea water still lingered in the back of my throat. I'd learned how to add towers to my castle with the plastic cup I'd filled with perfect sand, not too wet and not too dry, so it slid perfectly out of the mould. I set about digging the moat with my plastic shovel, so the strongest waves could surround my proud edifice with water. They would arrive via a long, steep canal, then split into two channels and surround the castle walls. I watched for the precise moment when the right and left tributaries joined, for a few fractions of a second, before both were absorbed into the sand.

My mother was chatting with Mémie in the shade of the parasol on the cabin doorstep, as their voices lulled my cousin to sleep in his stroller. Just metres away, Nesrine had set up her deck chair and was keeping an eye on me, wetting my hair every half-hour to prevent sunstroke. As my mother had warned me, the sun was bad at that time of day. This was certainly one of her favourite phrases, one Fatheya also regularly borrowed, a token of her irrefutable loyalty and the dogged persistence with which she cared for my mother's son's well-being. I couldn't say exactly what time of day she was referring to; I was still of an age to always have a woman at my side, to worry about whether the sun was bad on my behalf.

Nesrine took a camera from her bag and motioned with her hand for me to look at her. I posed nobly in front of my castle, which was sinking catastrophically, eroded by the water's successive incursions. As Nesrine focused her camera, I saw my mother leap up from her deck chair and stride toward us. The wind in her sarong made her steps look even more nervous. She called out to her sister-in-law, who couldn't see her coming from behind.

'What exactly are you doing?'

Nesrine made a gesture to show she hadn't understood the question.

'And this?' she went on, pointing with her chin at the camera Nesrine wore around her neck.

'We're taking pictures, Mira. Why are you being like that?'

'It's to send to him, isn't it?'

Mira, Mira, blowing up. I was stupefied. Indifferent to me, they proceeded with their quarrel, of which I understood little save the identity of this *him*, which was clear even to six-year-old me. I could feel my heart pounding, dreading the moment when they would finally remember that I was there. I refrained from making the slightest sound, lest the blast hit me, too, until I saw Fatheya coming over. She was on her way back from the apartment and picked up the pace when she sensed the tension from a distance. When she was just a few metres away, I felt tears rising up. My throat constricted and I let out a plaintive, childish cry. Fatheya pretended to be excited about collecting shells along the seashore. When no one replied, she took me by the arm and led me away from the drama. I was even, uncharacteristically, allowed to walk along the shoreline, where the waves washed up. Perhaps because she didn't know how to swim, Fatheya was unusually terrified by the idea of me going for a dip. But she must have sensed that this would be our last chance to enjoy the sea. With each wave that washed over my ankle, I bent my toes to trap as much sand as possible under the soles of my feet.

When we got back to the others, my mother told me not to unpack: we were leaving for Cairo the next day. I don't know what they'd said to each other in my absence, but not one word was exchanged that evening. Mémie said she had a migraine and went to bed. My uncle was taciturn as ever. Nesrine didn't speak to my mother. My mother didn't say a word to anyone. My cousin dozed in his stroller. Oblivious to the tension in the air, he had been lulled into a deep and peaceful sleep by the sunshine and his lack of worldly cares and the plain fact of being three years old, with two parents living together and no understanding of a thing. A trickle of drool dribbled from his slack jaw. Someone would be sure to wipe it away later.

The rest of my summer vacation would be spent at the Wadi al-Nil scout camp in Heliopolis. In short pants and knee socks, with a scarf around my neck, I'd spend the summer saluting the flag in Arabic, washing dented plates, and training my bladder, which was put to the test by endless hikes. I would move my lips, pretending to know the songs, with their interchangeable lyrics, while I occupied my mind concocting schemes to avoid being signed up for this again the following summer. Even in your absence, you still managed to spoil my vacation.

30

Montreal, 2000

'Mail for you, doc.'

She speaks to him in English, without looking up. Even her jokes
somehow take on the impersonal tone of an administrative exchange.

'Three test results. And one love letter. It's about time you found
someone. A catch like you!'

When she breaks out in laughter, her face blossoms into expression, then
the laughter turns to coughing. She tries to stifle it, smother it in a blanket
of curses drawn from her truly bottomless fund, and then starts in on
him again.

'Take good care of her, doc! She's got lovely handwriting.'

The cough and laughter drift down the hallway, feeding off each
other and drowning out the squeaking of the mail-cart wheels. Each
exhalation sounds like the scraping out of the shovelfuls of tar deposited
in her airways by years of smoking.

'You take care, too, Viviane. And lay off the smokes!'

There are indeed three internal-mail envelopes with medical results
and one pale yellow handwritten envelope addressed to him. Tarek grabs
that one. The letter inside is written in Arabic.

Cairo, March 23, 2000

Dear Doctor,
Please allow me to introduce myself: I'm a freelance journalist
working on a story about Egyptian doctors around the world,
and I'd like to talk to you. Could you spare a moment to
learn a little more about my project?

I would be most grateful if you would consider it.

Sincerely,
Ahmed Naguib

*The handwriting is neat, the paper free of letterhead. A crease forms on
his forehead as he reads. It is less the sender's name, which means nothing
to him, than the sight of the Arabic characters forming the name of his
hometown, Cairo, that causes his face to cloud over. He doesn't read it
again, just calmly crumples it up and throws it in his wastebasket.*

31

Cairo, 1998

Two years had gone by. Two years spent trying to piece together your life as a phantom progenitor, when the mere mention of your name was taboo. Fatheya was still telling me her stories of you, one drop at a time. She would meticulously select the most relatable-seeming snippets, generously peppering each new version with details that were, if not exactly incoherent, at the very least unnecessary. I was beginning to tire of her stories, which seemed to be more about her than you. Increasingly, they sounded like dubious excuses for me to keep her company. There were a few photos of you that had miraculously escaped my mother's purifying zeal. They showed a tall man with dark hair, sunken cheeks, and a slightly hooked nose. It was hard to see the resemblance from one photo to the next, and I tired of poring over the pictures to find traits you might have shared with me. I had the letters, sent by a man whose identity was even more elusive than the small specks of you I had painstakingly gathered. I had so little. When I was about to give up on reworking my patchwork of scraps, an incident occurred that changed everything.

My diligence at school had placed me among the 'good students,' the ones who don't make waves. One teacher, who thought I was ahead of my classmates, had even suggested to my mother that I skip a grade. She refused out of hand. Her obsession with being *like everyone else* made it inconceivable that I should stray from the beaten path in any way. Mira, Mira, over and out. My grandmother agreed, albeit for different reasons: she felt it was better for me to be the best in my level than an average student in a higher grade. Her sole comment on my precociousness was enigmatic: *The apple never falls far from the tree.* It felt more like a compliment to herself than to me.

To please my mother and grandmother, I made a point of earning high marks and otherwise passing unnoticed. At the end of the year, a good third of the class still didn't know my name. I'd given up trying to find common ground with my classmates, and begun taking comfort in their indifference. But I wasn't prepared for how Fatheya would deal with my hormonal changes.

Obsessed with the peach fuzz that had sprouted on my upper lip, she had been on a months-long campaign to get me to shave. She assured me that I could expect her full logistical and moral support, whenever I was ready. It came more as an announcement than a suggestion. I was hesitant. Unlike Fatheya, I was far from thrilled by the prospect of this male ritual. As far as I could tell, shaving seemed to bring more discomfort than satisfaction. Above all, it felt like unleashing a vicious cycle, as attested by the endless supply of halva Fatheya prepared for my mother's sugar waxing. The groans that emerged from the secrecy of the bathroom requisitioned for that purpose were among the most agonizing mysteries of my childhood.

Fatheya took the lead. Sick and tired of my procrastinating, she gave me a bottle of Chabrawichi 555 for my fourteenth birthday. One morning she came to greet me when I awoke, having retained the increasingly annoying habit of entering my room without knocking.

'Happy birthday, Rafik!'

'It's in two months … '

'I know, honey, but you were born in July. And my gift can't wait until the end of the school year.'

From the ring of flowers adorning the label, I at first mistook the bottle for some sort of cleaning product and tried to mask my confusion with a polite thank-you. But it would take more than that to dampen Fatheya's enthusiasm.

'This is the best cologne in the world! Every man I've ever known has worn it!' she said, punching *every* to stress the statistical validity of her argument. She paused with a serious look on her face, as if scrolling through a mental list of her conquests to recall each one's scent. Thrown off guard by this confidence, I hadn't seen Fatheya reach for the bottle and unleash a generous spray into the air. She sealed her argument with a white lie.

'Your father put this on every morning after his shower!'

Fatheya's gift was not without ulterior motives. She clearly hoped the cologne would encourage me to shave for the first time. Unless stolen from one of the apparently numerous men she had been intimate with, the bottle must have represented a substantial investment for Fatheya. Feeling guilty for not having shown suitable gratitude, I relented. I was ready to face the ordeal of the razor. Fatheya didn't have to be asked twice. I immediately found myself on the edge of the bathtub with the bottom half of my face lathered up with white foam from a shaving brush she had pulled out of God knows where.

'Now what?'

'Now you shave!'

'Like this?'

'Hey, Goha! Where's your ear?'

It was one of her favourite jokes, a reference to the popular movie character who, when asked to touch his right ear, stretched his left hand over his head. Fatheya meant that I always found ways to complicate a simple situation. She quickly turned the razor I'd been holding upside down and pressed her large, rough fingers against mine, to begin the first movement. The result was satisfactory. No cuts, which would have been a crushing failure. At most, a few beads of blood here and there. These she atomized with Chabrawichi 555, in much the same relentless way she sprayed Baygon on any cockroach reckless enough to cross her path in the kitchen. I remember the sting of alcohol on my irritated skin, and Fatheya's three slaps on my cheek, meant to seal the operation.

'Go on. Go show your mother that you're a man now!'

As it happened, my mother didn't notice my close shave, only the overpowering scent of my new fragrance. She took exaggerated deep breaths, pretending to analyze what was different in the air. I knew she was just trying to find the right words to make fun of this addition to my grooming routine. Mira, Mira, ever sarcastic. I immediately told her the cologne was a present from Fatheya, and that I was late for school. Unassailable arguments, both.

I'd just missed the school bus, which meant taking the city bus to Collège de la Sainte-Famille on the Nile's other bank. After jogging the last few metres, I got to class as the teacher was taking attendance. As my name hadn't been called yet, I was able to take my seat with no more than a scolding look.

I'd been assigned to share a desk with an especially wild boy, in keeping with the age-old Jesuit custom of placing disruptive and well-behaved students side by side. The idea was that one would inspire a thirst for redemption in the other. I could not in all honesty recall a single case where this had worked, but there must have been a few in the history of the Collège de la Sainte-Famille to justify the method's popularity. My classmate Sherif's main claim to fame was that, alone among us, he had already gone through puberty. He wasn't precocious, he had repeated two grades. This lent him a certain legitimacy as a gang leader and also, if he were to be believed, great success with girls.

I had only just caught my breath after my sprint to class, and it took a while to realize that his taunt was directed at me. He waited for the bell to ring before calling me out, for all to hear.

'Hey, looking good!'

(Ignore it, let it pass.)

'Who'd you get all prettied up for?'

(He shouldered me, to make me look. Don't react, wait until he gets bored.)

'Did you put on *perfume* this morning? Maybe you're a fag like your father?'

The punch threw itself. I'd never been in a fight before, and wouldn't have thought I had it in me, but the inspiration came to me all on its own. Here I should mention that I wasn't fully clear on the meaning of the term. At best I knew where it ranked in the hierarchy of schoolyard insults, and that alone was enough to spur retaliation. I curled my fingers into a fist and punched Sherif in the face. Caught somewhere between disbelief and fascination, the other students backed away to form a cautious semicircle around us. They started cheering loudly. Sherif grabbed my uniform shirt to throw me to the ground, but tripped and fell before he could pull it off. I used this reprieve to strike a second blow, but he blocked my fist with the palm of his hand. I'm sure he would have crushed it, had a teacher not come over to break us up and march us to the principal's office, in a chorus of whistling from our classmates. My school was unaccustomed to such scenes. With a three-day suspension, I felt I had gotten off easy.

The episode earned me my mother's rebukes and Fatheya's congratulations. To the former, I was careful not to mention your role in the fight; to the latter, I left out the part played by Chabrawichi 555.

'You did the right thing; I'm sure he deserved a beating! And on the same day you shaved! I knew it would make a man of you!'

Fatheya proudly pinched my cheek before continuing.

'Now don't go doing that every day, hey? You do it once, to show them what you're made of. But don't go turning into a tough! Anyway, I know one person who won't bother you again … '

'Faty, was my father a fag?'

The question had been running around in my head all day. I now saw that part of the aura of mystery surrounding you was related to that word, but I didn't want to ask Fatheya what it meant at the risk of having her make something up. I was bluffing. I saw her eyes widen.

'Is that what your fight was about?'

'Answer my question … '

I could tell my question had caught Fatheya off guard, but she quickly recovered. First, she criticized me for using that word in front of a lady. Next, she admonished me for paying attention to schoolyard gossip. I let her sink into her distractions, never once taking my eyes off her. I could sense her trying to separate the wheat of what I really knew from the chaff of my bluff, and I was taking pains not to reveal the slightest clue. Eventually, she lost her temper and unleashed a string of profanities, cursing out everyone she could think of. To my surprise, Ali's name was added to her litany.

'What does Ali have to do with it?'

Alert to my surprise, she hesitated. It was too late to change her mind. She'd never mentioned that name without my forcing her hand, and I could see the panic in her eyes. A wolf caught in a trap, when it realizes that there will be no getting out alive.

The few times I'd asked Fatheya about Ali, she'd always said the same thing. He was 'a young man with problems.' And you'd had the foolish idea of trying to help him. And I was to keep quiet about it. *A young man with problems.* Behind that euphemism, I could sense that this young man was at the root of many of *our* problems, your leaving chief among them. Maybe he had problems of his own as well. I had never really thought about that. As for why he wrote you letters …

Now everything snapped into place: the meaning of the insult, your connection with Ali, the mysteries surrounding your departure. It was all so brutally obvious.

The day would come when I'd regret the spite that welled up inside me. I had the sudden feeling that the universe was not vast enough to contain my anger, which was out of all proportion to the one that had made me fight two hours earlier.

I now began to hate my peers without discrimination. The ones whose fathers' status meant they needed no introduction, gave them a sense of accomplishment before they'd even lived. The ones born with a clear model they merely had to replicate to become men of consequence. The ones who had grown up beside the spring and drank from it without having known thirst.

I hated my family for concealing from me a truth known to everyone else. As if hiding all mirrors were enough to protect a deformed being from its own ugliness.

Most of all, I hated you.

You, who up to now I had cursed for not being there, I now cursed for existing. Because of you, I was the son of a man who had slept with a man. I was the son of a man who had abandoned his wife. I was the laughing stock of my class. I was the last idiot who didn't know who I was.

It was all a jumble in my head. I didn't understand what I hated; I hated what I didn't understand.

With a nervous jerk I knocked over the contents of my desk. Fatheya tried to reason with me, begging me not to breathe a word of this conversation. She would lose her job … I didn't listen. I yelled at her to get out of my room. She left. For weeks silence reigned between us.

32

Cairo, 1999

Mémie passed away. I was fifteen and had never seen death up so close. The experience was not without a certain excitement.

I'd seen the sympathy and compassion lavished on my classmates when they told their teachers of the loss of a loved one. But I had received only knowing looks – sometimes mocking, sometimes reproachful – when it came to you. It was night and day. My school-yard fight the year before had made the subject even more painful to me. For a long time I resented you for not being dead. An orphaned child is pure, an abandoned child shameful. By entitling me to the pity you had denied me, my grandmother's death redressed a certain injustice. At last, I could be pitied without qualification.

I can say this now, but I know she would have reproached me for it: Mémie resolutely stood against self-pity in all shapes and forms. 'Those who flaunt their misfortune will never inspire desire or fear' was among my grandmother's guiding principles, one of the abiding and incontrovertible truths to which she held the secret. 'It's just the way of the world,' she would baldly state, as if to dissuade anyone from even trying to question her assertion. She had the merit of consistency: even when it came to you, I never once saw my grandmother bemoan her fate.

She had died of *what she had*. I could never say what exactly that was, but toward the end our family life had been arranged around this death foretold. Everything fell into one of two fundamental and mutually exclusive categories: what was bad for *what she had* and everything else. When *what she had* made her long-feared demise inevitable, she summoned us in order – Nesrine, Mira, me, and then Fatheya – to deliver her last words.

I have to admit that I'd hoped for more. I'd expected some sort of earth-shattering revelation – ideally about you – but instead had to be content with a series of platitudes about the meaning of honour, the meaning of family, and ensuring that the affliction soon to befall us, her death, would open no opportunity for the maid to make off with our valuables. As parting words go, they were paltry and mean. I was leaving her room, thinking our final conversation would not be among my most memorable with my grandmother, when I saw Fatheya, prostrate on a chair, awaiting her turn. She was a picture of inner torment. Kohl-blackened tears fell from tired eyes. Her employer herself could not have wished for more poignant drama. It has to be said that, since that morning, Fatheya had made her own list of a thousand reasons for this summons. Each had been mentally reviewed, from the best-case scenario – a share of the inheritance in recognition of her skilled and dutiful service – to the most terrifying, a dismissal impossible not to see as wrongful. The moment she saw me leave, she leapt to her feet and rushed into the dying woman's room.

Mémie simply asked her to dial her son's phone number, leave the room, and stay nearby in case the line went dead. She was further asked not to eavesdrop on the door, 'just this once,' a comment history will record as my grandmother's final callous act toward Fatheya.

❧

Up till then, my inner circle had been touched even less by death than by change, which is saying a lot. I had begun to wonder whether the same women who had bent over my cradle would one day stand over my grave. In a sense, Mémie's passing restored the natural order of things. I wouldn't want you to think, when you read this, that her death didn't devastate me; nothing could be further from the truth. The mainstay of the Holy Trinity of women that made up my family was no more. I fell into a deep distress.

Truth be told, I've always felt I owed my very presence in this family to Mémie. I can only believe my pregnant and recently abandoned mother must have stopped wanting me, must have considered all her options – to let herself wither away with what was left of you in her womb, or to wait for my birth to drop me off at the first available orphanage. In the only version I can imagine, her mother-in-law must have intervened to convince her to keep me. Of course, I have no proof, but the thought has always brought me closer to Mémie. I can't think of a single happy childhood memory without her. She probably knew how to read me better than my own mother.

I had just lost the one who would cheer me up with sweet aish al-Saraya picked up from Mandarine Koueider. The one who had always maintained a subtle preference for me over my cousin, as if to counterbalance the injustice of our fates. The one who could read a glorious future for me in the grounds of the Turkish coffee I forced myself to drink for the sake of hearing her predictions. She would flip over my blackened cup and frown, the better to decipher the clues in the patterns the grounds left behind, and then deliver her verdict. These futures always involved efforts to be made, challenges to be overcome, and a brilliant destiny befitting of my strength of character. How could it be otherwise? After all, I was born on the July 14, Bastille Day – national holiday of the greatest country in the world. As if in confirmation of her portent, she sometimes even saw the French flag in the grounds. Without a shadow of a doubt, a bright future awaited me.

On those rare occasions when Mémie forgot herself and spoke your name in my presence, I saw a flutter in her eyes. Clearly aware of the taboo she had unwittingly broken, she would try to gauge the severity of the breach. It wasn't as if she had only now revealed to me that she had a son and I had a father, and that these two were one and the same person. But I could see that it bothered her. I gave her my most indifferent look, to reassure her that I hadn't heard anything shocking, or even anything at all, and she could go on with her story without it seeming suspicious. At other times I'd let her silences speak, telling me about you. I'd ask her a question straight up, one I knew concerned you, affecting a childlike inno-cence to lend my query an innocuous air. Was it easier to raise a boy or a girl? What had been her life's greatest hardship to date? She would remain silent, think long and hard. Knowing that you alone were on her mind at that moment, I would try to catch a glimpse of you beneath those expressive wrinkles. She'd find a diver-sion to manoeuvre our conversation through this minefield. It didn't matter. Without exchanging a word, in the space between my falsely naive questions and her dissembling answer, we talked about you. These non-conversations of ours were one more thing I would miss.

My mother, too, was adept at dodging questions about you. When someone would ask me one, she'd jump in to answer. *His father's not here anymore* ... Then she would lower her eyes, to sow just the right amount of confusion and discourage further questions. *Not here anymore* may not have meant much, but it was at least better than *gone abroad because he never got over the death of his lover, a prostitute garbage-picker's son.* For all we knew, you were dead. In support of this thesis, she never failed to add, *We're blessed to live with my mother-in-law, she's so wonderful!* This final bit was proof that there was nothing untoward in our situation. It was simply one of those tragedies to be faced with courage rather than opprobrium. Mira, Mira, prevaricating.

I'd never been particularly close to my other grandparents. When they insisted on speaking to me in their own language, I'd pretend not to understand or I'd answer in Arabic, taking a cruel childish pleasure in their appalled faces at my failure to be Armenian. Spending time with them gave me an experience of the same tension between familiarity and foreignness that they never stopped feeling with Egypt. With Mémie now gone, I at first feared that I'd have to move into their home. It seemed somehow outside the natural order to imagine my mother and I living on our own, with no higher authority to make the big decisions for us. In retrospect, I should perhaps have been more surprised that my mother lived with her mother-in-law to the end. But it certainly gave everyone what they needed: for your mother, the guarantee of seeing me grow up, even after your departure; for mine, a modicum of the social stability she held so dear.

I soon learned that we would not be dispensing with the family apartment or Fatheya's services. That came as a relief. I didn't feel equal to the task of soaking up the ambient melancholy of my mother's daily life single-handedly. Pretending to ignore her bouts of bulimia. Artificially filling the void left by the two great departures, first yours and then your mother's. For my adolescent self, that would all have been too much.

Surprisingly, it hadn't entered my mind that you might come to Mémie's funeral. You'd always existed in a reality that ran parallel to my own, and I'd accepted the geometrical precept that parallel lines never meet. It took Fatheya to sow doubt in my mind. *I mean, he could have come to see her before she died. Wouldn't that be the normal thing to do?* In our family, *normal* was not a compelling argument. Then Fatheya said something that plunged me into an ocean of possibilities.

'What about the funeral? Do you think he'll come back?'

'He didn't come back to see her when she was alive. And you expect him to come now that she's dead? Seriously?'

I felt the hypothesis warranted more serious consideration than being waved away with a rhetorical backhand. I decided, for once, to test it out on my mother. She responded with a puzzled fluttering of her eyelids and asked who had gone and put an idea like that in my head. I could have pointed a finger at Fatheya, but it was better not to incriminate anyone. She had just been released from my grandmother's clutches, and I would feel bad turning her new employer against her.

'Go write your speech for Mémie's mass instead.'

She was staring at me with the expression of a parent weary of having to tuck in a child grown too old to believe in ghosts. It was best not to push my luck. I took her advice and went back to my eulogy. There wasn't much time left to write, especially in the elegant formal French that would have pleased Mémie. My grandmother may have spent most of her life in Egypt, but her Khawageya accent had never ceased to deform the Arabic language. As far as I knew, she regularly spoke Arabic only to the doorman, the water deliveryman, and of course Fatheya – no one who would inspire her to perfect her command. Nesrine was much better, even if there came a point in every conversation when you could tell it wasn't her mother tongue. I had grown comfortable living in two languages: French in the classroom and at home, Arabic in the playground. Since Mémie viewed the two languages as rivals, and her own preference was unmistakable, I would watch local TV when no one was looking and then flip over to TV5Monde the moment I heard her coming. She expected me to speak *with style* and never thought twice about forcing me to rephrase a sentence to correctly use the imperfect subjunctive. When I tried to find out more about her definition of *style*, she gave me an enigmatic look.

'Errors of agreement or spelling don't matter, so long as they aren't *lapses of taste*! Don't the Jesuits teach you that? Just look at all these adverbs. Do you really need them all? There: a fine example of a *lapse of taste*!'

I didn't always understand the meaning of her words of wisdom, but I knew when to give her an understanding smile to suggest the very opposite. She sometimes asked me to recite one of the three or four texts she'd made me memorize. She was especially fond of one Victor Hugo poem about a child being punished with dry bread whose grandfather brings her a clandestine jar of jam. I couldn't imagine Mémie condoning such behaviour in real life. But she seemed more outraged by my poor pronunciation of the word *confiture* than the old man's fraught relationship with authority. Looking back now, it strikes me that she was always much more indulgent with those living in her imagined France than with her own offspring.

'One day,' she used to promise me, 'we'll go to Paris!'

Although it never happened, I do believe she sincerely meant to. She had gotten to know the city on a trip with her own parents and spoke of it with an enthusiasm I rarely saw in her. She closed her eyes and rocked her head, as if her move was needed to summon her memories.

Sous le ciel de Paris
S'envole une chanson
Elle est née d'aujourd'hui
Dans le cœur d'un garçon …

Her singing was slightly off-key, her voice deeper than usual, and her gaze was meant to convey dreams of Parisian grandeur.

I never knew my grandmother's real first name until a few days after her death, when her obituary came back from the printer's. She had always been called Tante Aimée by cousins and close friends, but her real name turned out to be Amal. To a name that meant *hope* she had preferred to be Aimée, loved. I let my mind run with the metaphor.

I was sitting at my desk, struggling to form sentences in the one language fit for a tribute to my grandmother, when Fatheya burst into my room. Her heavy breathing made it clear that she wasn't in the habit of running up and down stairs.

'Is everything all right?'

She closed the door and used her body to keep it locked, both hands firmly gripping the handle behind her back.

'You were right!'

'What are you talking about?'

'You were right about Tarek! He's coming.'

I let her talk. I didn't want to get ahead of myself: it was such a serious subject, and Fatheya was known to jump to conclusions. She went on.

'Remember when you asked me, you know, if your father was coming? I didn't believe it at the time, but it got me thinking. Then I saw Nesrine heading toward your mother's room. She looked preoccupied, and God, blessed be his name, told me to follow her. Then I heard everything! I'm sure your mother will come tell you the news, any second. But I'd rather you had time to digest it first … '

This wasn't the first time that God-blessed-be-his-name had ordered Fatheya to eavesdrop, but I knew what had driven her to tell me this new information: her pride at being the first to know. I didn't interrupt.

'The two of them started talking. I couldn't hear very well, and it was mostly in French anyway, but they were saying your father's name, so of course I kept listening! And at one point, they mentioned the airport … '

'Airport? Are you sure they said *airport*?'

Fatheya let go of the door handle and held out her hand to me, her palm extended theatrically upward. In it, a sheet of paper, not easily prised from her clammy grasp. I unfolded it and recognized my mother's handwriting in a series of characters.

'What's this?'

'What does it look like? The flight number!'

'Is it from my mother's notebook?'

'Of course it is!'

She said the words with the triumphant air of a dog with a stick of dynamite. I made her say it again.

'Faty, is this page torn from my mother's notebook?'

'Yes, it's from your mother's notebook. Seriously, is that all you have to say to me? That'll teach me to come and … '

I stared at her in disbelief. She suddenly grasped the implications of the situation.

'Oh shit! I've torn a page from your mother's notebook!'

My mind was racing. First we had to get our hands on that notebook; then we could come up with some sort of plan. Fatheya was slumped on my bed, wild-eyed and leaden-faced. Since she hadn't registered a word of what I said, I decided to go sort it out myself.

When my mother came into my room, I pretended to be too absorbed in my work to notice her preoccupied expression. She was about to say something when she saw her notebook, which I was busy writing in.

'I was looking for that … '

'Oh? Sorry, I needed some paper for Mémie's speech.'

I put on my most detached air. She took her notebook. She looked at me without really listening, as if the truth was more likely to be found in my face than in my words. She sat down on the edge of my bed, where Fatheya's posterior had left a concentric mark of crumpled fabric, and scrolled through the sheets pressed under her thumb until she came to the blank pages.

'I'd written something down. Did you happen to see it?'

I looked for the wastebasket and uncrumpled the balls of paper one by one. Soon I found the sheet Fatheya had torn out. I'd carefully crossed out the writing on the other side of the page, to make it look like just another draft of my eulogy. As I handed it to her, I felt the relief loosening the tightness in her brow.

All was back in order. My mother was now free to announce your arrival, an opportunity that would never come again. At the same time, she could explain the meaning of the mysterious series of letters and numbers I had pretended to discover and rescue *in extremis* from the wastebasket. She, who had prohibited her family from revealing my existence to you, could now be the one to tell me I was finally going to meet you.

My heart was under pressure, like the pots of stuffed cabbage Fatheya covered with a plate weighted down by a heavy stone. I suppressed the pounding, prepared to meet my mother's news with the greatest possible detachment. I even feigned indifference to facilitate her task. Surely she was also trying to mask her feelings just as I was, for her face was a blank slate. Clearly, each of us was trying to protect ourselves from the other, while my mother struggled to find the words that would forever change our lives.

33

Montreal, 2000

When he comes into the office, he first takes off his gloves, then grabs a brown paper towel from the dispenser to mop his forehead. The fluorescent light flickers and buzzes, briefly emitting a pallid glow before fully turning on. He rests his inert hands under a trickle of water for a good while before vigorously scrubbing them with liquid soap. He pulls out a new paper towel, dries his fingers, and at last collapses in his desk chair. His whole body seems to release in an interminable exhalation. Each moment of relaxation after a lengthy surgical procedure carries its own particular flavour.

A pale yellow envelope lies on his desk. He opens it with a scissor blade. A passport photo has come unclipped from the journalist's resumé. It is a photograph of a young man, with the deckled edges of a professional portrait. He seems unsurprised to discover the letter, written in Arabic, that accompanies it.

Cairo, June 2, 2000

Dear Doctor,
Perhaps you received my previous letter. If so, I apologize in advance for my insistence. My name is Ahmed Naguib and I'd like to talk to you for a story I am writing on doctors from our country. It would be a great honour to discuss

your career, and your father's as well. Would you be so kind as to give me a few moments of your time in the coming weeks?

He looks out of his office window. It's 8:13 p.m., and the skyscrapers are reflecting the last rays of the sun. The days are lengthening as spring draws to an end, as if they still have more to reveal. He writes a few words on the back of the photo, then crumples the letter and resumé into a ball that lands in the garbage can on the first throw. Viviane catches his triumphant smile.

'Nice shot, doc! Your prize is the rest of the night off.'

He doesn't pick up on her sarcasm, just nods his thanks.

'What, that love letter didn't do it for you? You're tough on the suitors!'

'Not even warm, Viviane,' *he says, handing her the photo of the young man.*

'Right ... He's pretty good-looking, though. If I was fifteen years younger ... '

'Fifteen? You're getting younger! I'd say he's barely twenty.'

She mutters a few unintelligible syllables and then clears her throat.

'Do you know him?'

'No, he's a journalist. I wouldn't put much stock in his articles, though. He has that obsequious tone of an Egyptian getting ready to ask you for money.'

'You're hard on your country, doctor ... '

'It was hard on me.'

She hesitates a moment before getting started again.

'You threw away his letter but kept his photo?'

'It's a superstition. You should never throw out someone's photo. Or tear it up. No one ever told you that?'

'Still, though ... Is that normal, in your country? To send a photo when you want to write an article?'

He shrugs. Viviane discreetly takes her leave. He doesn't notice. He turns off the light and locks his office door. As he walks out of the Royal Victoria Hospital's main entrance, he stops to wave at the two interns taking a break in front of the deserted reception desk. He stops for a moment, close enough to the building that he can still catch wafts of the chemicals used to sterilize the hospital. He seems poised to turn back, but then sticks to his original route, crosses the parking lot, and exits the hospital grounds.

On University Street he takes in the last views of Mount Royal before it blends in with the city. Houses stand on rocky outcroppings, as if oblivious to the slope supporting them. He gazes absent-mindedly at their ivied facades. The breeze is warm, it's snowing pollen. His feet carry him to the McGill University campus entrance. Students sit in clusters on the grass or stroll nonchalantly along. They are pictures of carefree youth, with book bags over their shoulders. He glimpses a group lining up at the door of one of the buildings. Out of curiosity, he walks over to the poster on the glass door. It advertises a presentation in English. Entangled photons and other mysteries of quantum physics. *He has nothing else to do that evening.*

34

Cairo, 1999

'Nothing at all? Not even a hint?'

Fatheya was ordering her thoughts, instinctively nodding her head. To avoid arousing suspicion, she had been closely monitoring my aunt's and mother's comings and goings, to determine the best time for our rendezvous. My aunt had gone home, and my mother was on the phone with her mother. We'd have a good half-hour. It felt like a scene from one of those daytime TV programs they show during Ramadan, to keep people occupied until they can break fast.

'She must have said something, Rafik. Think!'

'She just asked me how far along I was on my speech for the service.'

'What about the paper?'

'Well ... since she didn't mention it, I waited awhile and then asked her. She said it was the number of something she'd ordered, from Europe.'

'Rafik, I swear to you before the Most High that I heard her say – '

'I know you did. I called the airport. They confirmed that it was a flight number. From Montreal. Arriving tomorrow.'

While it didn't satisfy her, the confirmation gave Fatheya food for thought. Two things were now clear: one, you were coming for the funeral, and two, my mother was deliberately hiding it from me. After a long pause, Fatheya presented a final hypothesis, trying her best to formulate it in the way that would hurt the least.

'Say he knows he has a son … He might have asked your mother not to tell you he'd be there. You know, so as not to upset you … '

'And then what? Do you really think he expects to go unnoticed after being gone for fifteen years? C'mon, Faty, stop it. My mother was the one who insisted that I read a speech at her mass. She was the one who was ready to make up all kinds of stories to hide the flight number. She's trying to humiliate him, by having him find out about me on the day of his mother's funeral.'

Powerless before my unimpeachable logic, Fatheya stopped trying to argue. She pressed her palms together, as if she felt a headache coming on, and muttered.

'You've always thought like an adult. I don't know where your childhood went … '

I'd had a few hours longer than Fatheya to come to these conclusions and eliminate all other possible explanations for my mother's behaviour. A few hours to take the measure of my mother's reheated bitterness and the appetite for revenge that had fed on it. An impression, perhaps, of having been cheated out of her life. And was that not something I myself had felt?

I blamed my mother. She could have opted to pool her anger and mine, bringing us closer together. Instead, she had chosen to make me the instrument of a selfish revenge. The way she had raised me over the years was like patiently honing a knife, a weapon that gave the person wielding it just one chance to hit its target. I was no longer a child in her eyes. Unbeknownst to me, I had become a man: a man like the one who had shattered her dreams, a man who would only leave her in the end after all. A man it was better to sacrifice. Mira, Mira, striking first.

In my anger and despair, I thought back to Mémie. She never would have let this happen. I saw that these last few hours had been a misunderstanding – she was only now, at this exact moment, taking leave of this world. Now my mourning could begin. I imagined myself in the church, reading out my speech before the eyes of a roomful of people who had already recognized you and were waiting in complicit silence to watch this tragedy unfold. Instead of protecting me, my mother was forcing me to draft the indictment for a trial that had been waiting on the docket for fifteen years. I was no more than a collateral victim, a fool spending his life describing his pain for people far away. Hatred filled me up again. The queen was dead but not buried, and the chess game only just beginning. When it came, there would be carnage: no winners, only losers.

I pounded my clenched fist against the wall. Fatheya grabbed my arm to hold it back. She managed to restrain me. I let myself fall against her, unable to get a word out. I had cut the phalanx of one of my fingers. Blood was gushing out, preferring this sudden light to the prison of my veins. Inert, I watched it slowly drain away, joining a tendon to form a scarlet furrow, before drying out. I wept with rage. I was exhausted. I was a thousand years old.

Our hours were numbered. Nothing could be left to chance. I skipped the evening meal and spent the next morning in silent brooding, answering questions with a shake of my head. My mother put my silence down to grief, and that suited me fine. To get her to let her guard down, I showed her the speech I'd written for the funeral. She read it in silence, her lips scarcely moving. She smiled, then ended her reading with a guarded *very good*, before running a hand through my hair the way one might pet a dog to get it primed for a hunt. Her eyes betrayed no hint of remorse. It didn't matter, my energy was elsewhere. As luck would have it, Aunt Nesrine was there to finalize funeral preparations, drawing attention away from me. Being ignored left me time to hatch my plan, away from prying eyes, walled up in a fortress of silence to which only Fatheya held the key. She'd been asked to tidy up the Dokki apartment in preparation for the arrival, that very day, of a 'relative' come to attend the funeral. Of course she had not asked who it would be.

There remained one unknown: Would Nesrine come looking for you? Would she take you back up to Mémie's apartment? Our answer came when your arrival time drew near and no one stirred. As Mémie used to do when visitors arrived from abroad, I called the airport, the one from which she and I would never set off on our trip to Paris. Your plane was on time. At the moment you should have been stepping out onto the tarmac, no one had left the house. Evidently no one would be there to greet you. I was getting ready to leave for the Dokki apartment, with Ali's letters carefully filed in a sealed portfolio, in chronological order. They were my sacred relic, my sole tangible link to you. I felt a twinge of sorrow at the thought of parting with them, but they would be traded for a far more precious commodity. In them, Ali often mentioned his mother, so I planned a detour to buy a bowl of umm Ali. When you found the letters next to the dessert, you'd understand the intention behind the *mise en scène*. I had entrusted Fatheya with the outline of my plan, and she would cover for me if anyone was surprised by my absence. She gave me a hug as I left the house. I was already elsewhere.

35

Right up to her last days, Mémie was fond of regaling me with pearls of her wisdom, based on the proud example of her own life. She would clothe these precepts in a handful of dubious aphorisms and present them, somewhat pompously, as her 'philosophy.' Hers was a 'social' science, insofar as its sole aim was to make her sparkle in society, and the force of her maxims was meant to compensate for any lack of empirical evidence. As was to be expected, diction had pride of place. She never spoke of *chance*, preferring the word *fate*, which conveyed the same notion but with an added *noblesse*. For a long time this distinction struck me as mere pedantry, but I now see that the nuance was important. Not being in the habit of siding with losers, Mémie had found in *fate* a trusted ally to help her be certain of always landing on the winning side. Fate justified trials and tribulations and stamped the winners with the impress of divine election; *chance* reduced defeat to poor planning and victory to dumb luck. And what power do we have against fate? Mémie's answer to this rhetorical question never varied: *none*. In Arabic, Mektoub. All has been written, our role is merely to play the notes on a score revealed as we go, so what is to come remains as inscrutable as the melody they will form together. For my grandmother, who had devoted so much of her life to the weaving and unravelling of schemes and machinations, fate was no mere superstition but an inestimable alibi.

Though they aroused no particular enthusiasm in me, when I saw Mémie proudly expounding her theories, I made sure my eyes expressed just the right amount of support to keep her going. Her talks struck a balance between warning and self-reflection, and tended to end in resignation.

'You know, Rafik, trying to change the future is pointless at best. And at worst, you risk displeasing the Good Lord.' I should clarify that, while Mémie's God was not to be crossed with impunity, the qualifier *good* referred not to any alleged mercy but rather to the fact that, unlike most of her country, she had had the clairvoyance to choose the right heavenly interlocutor.

On the night before her funeral, I wondered whether I might have antagonized Mémie's Good Lord in my attempts to get close to you. When you pushed me violently aside in the street, without the slightest suspicion of who I might be, I momentarily regretted not having paid more heed to my grandmother's superstitions. What did I hope to achieve with these letters, with this *mise en scène*? From what depths had I summoned the arrogance to think I could anticipate your reactions when I knew nothing about you? I'd tried to speed up time, to force a meeting before its moment. Soon I would pay for my rashness.

I prepared for the funeral with the numb affect and robotic gait of a condemned man making his way to the gallows. In my hand I held the sheet of paper with the eulogy I would soon have to read in front of you. I would have been happy if Mémie's wrathful god smote me, here in the privacy of my room, but he seemed intent on a public execution. I felt desperately alone. I could barely find the words to tell Fatheya what had happened at our first meeting. Or, rather, what had not.

At the church I was confronted with the wooden coffin in which my grandmother had been laid to rest. It seemed inordinately small. I could have sworn that it was shorter than my outstretched arms, but never got the chance to check. A parade of saints adorned the monumental iconostasis that separated the nave from the sanctuary. Their faces were ominous as they watched over Mémie in her box. Certainly, they knew all there was to know of the scene about to play out in front of them. I searched for clues in the fullness of their countenances, but they revealed nothing. Drugged with incense, draped in a holy hypocrisy, they feigned indifference.

The church was filling up. The men were carefully dressed, the women radiantly grief-stricken. In outpourings of empathy, they laid hands on my head. What right did my grief give them to run their fingers through my hair? At the very least, it entitled me to not smile back. Every black satin gown in Cairo was in those wooden pews. The priest smiled, intoxicated by the sight of his large and well-heeled flock. It occurred to me that Mémie wouldn't have missed such a gathering for the world; then again, even in death, she had managed to make herself the centre of attention.

Now that I knew what you looked like, I turned around from time to time to see whether you'd arrived. I tried not to think about the moment I'd be called up to the lectern to read my speech. How would I look when the priest introduced me as your son? Which of us would be more humiliated? Would you see that I was the boy who had tried to approach you in the street the day before? The church was now full. I gave up looking for you in the densely packed crowd. I felt trapped, like the Mamluk chiefs besieged in the Cairo citadel a century earlier. An image they'd shown us on a school trip had always stuck with me: a stone split by a horse's hoof. It conveyed the desperation of the rider who had thrown himself from the ramparts, preferring a death of his own choosing to one imposed by someone else. At that moment, I would have swapped my tawdry kingdom for a horse.

The ceremony began with a drawn-out organ note. Maman whispered a few words in Nesrine's ear, and we all took our seats in the front row. The priest intoned the opening, his deep voice singing out the usual improvised litany. Why follow the score when the Word of God is with you? You must have been standing a metre from me, stunned by the same unmelodic lament. That much at least we shared. The thought was almost enough to lessen my despair. I wasn't listening to the words of the ceremony. What could I possibly have learned about my grandmother? I knew her better than anyone else in that church, except perhaps you. Yet you and I did not share a single memory of her.

The curls of incense seemed to dance around the coffin that would soon be interred, only to disappear a metre from our heads, releasing their potent scent – making no attempt to reach the gods, content instead to reassure us mere mortals. My mother grabbed my shoulders, like a drowsy child being woken up in class. It was my turn to speak. I walked up to the altar, took a moment to kneel, and crossed myself methodically. In the name of the Father, the Son. I climbed the few steps up to the pulpit, readjusted the microphone, and unfolded the text that had crumpled in my pocket. I sought out neither your gaze nor my mother's. I averted my eyes from that short box in which Mémie was now contorted. I let neither my emotion nor the incense seize my throat. I read my text without trembling. I was alone, as I had always been.

The expected cataclysm failed to materialize. Leaning over the pulpit, I felt no ripples unsettling the decorum of the assembled mourners. No one holding their breath with faces turned in your direction, no excited whispering or palpable unease; nothing at all. It was no different later when I left the church – just a few old ladies congratulating me on my speech, their eyes red with emotion, perhaps touched by the knowledge that the next eulogy could be their own. No trace of you.

A thousand hypotheses raced through my agitated mind. Could it be that the man I had seen downstairs in Mémie's apartment wasn't you after all? Who, then? Some distant relative with no idea why he had been greeted with a bowl of umm Ali and a stack of cryptic letters? But then what of the Montreal flight number? No, you must have been there in the audience when I read my eulogy. Unless you'd missed your plane?

I saw Fatheya at the church door. I rushed over to her.

'Faty, have you seen him?'

She nodded *yes*. My heart suddenly started beating again.

'Well, where is he, then? Why hasn't he come to talk to me? How did he react when I read my speech?'

'He didn't hear you, Rafik. I waited for him outside the church and told him not to go in.'

I didn't immediately realize that Fatheya had saved me from the moment I'd been dreading. Strangely, I felt neither relief nor gratitude. I took a long breath.

'Faty, I want to talk to him. Just for a few moments. I'll come up and see him for fifteen minutes. Fifteen, no more. After that, I won't ask you for a thing, promise – '

She cut me off.

'He's gone … '

'What do you mean, gone? Is he already at the airport?'

'No. Upper Egypt.'

She didn't wait for my question before giving me her two-word answer.

'Finding Ali.'

36

Montreal, 2000

He sits in front of his computer. Only his pupils are moving, horizontally across the screen.

He clenches his jaw, presses a single key for a long moment, then starts clattering away with both hands. He stops. Rereads what he has written one last time. Takes up a sheet of paper and starts writing from right to left. His gaze alternates between the screen and the paper. The writing is laborious, with a slant unusual for Arabic calligraphy. There is something almost childlike about it.

He tears off the first page, then starts again.

Montreal, July 21, 2000

Dear Sir,
I don't know how you obtained my contact information. I do not wish to be interviewed for your article, and therefore thank you kindly for not contacting me again.

Dr. Tarek Seidah

He rereads the letter one final time, then places it in an envelope. He opens a drawer in his desk and pulls out a photo. He looks at it for a moment, then turns it over and copies the address onto the envelope. The envelope is still sitting in a corner of his desk. He picks up where he left off.

37

Cairo, 1999

'My God, Fatheya! You haven't changed a bit ... '

Of course she had changed. You both had; no one could deny
that time had traced creases on your faces and in your minds. Your
words were your way of telling Fatheya that you had recognized
her at first sight. She beckoned you to go with her, away from the
entrance. You followed without asking questions. Even from outside,
you could hear the organ heralding the words of the Almighty, a
reminder to men that dust returns to dust. You preferred to stay
outside, feeling the March wind disperse Fatheya's perfume. It made
you feel decades younger. The same perfume, on an aging woman.
She moved with less confidence than before, her gait punctuated
by little sighs she let out unawares. Of course she'd changed.

She asked how long you'd been here. You felt like a child caught
doing something bad, at once ashamed and relieved not to be carrying the secret alone. She told you your family had missed you. It
wasn't a reproach. The words made no attempt to imply more than
they said, they were enough in themselves.

'Mira suffered the most. She didn't deserve this, Tarek. She's a
good girl, you should have talked things over with her. That's what
you do when things aren't going well, you talk. You talk to people!
You try to fix what can be salvaged. You don't just leave ... '

You were about to start justifying yourself, but she lowered her
eyelids to let you know there was no need.

'Did you see? The letters?'

'Fatheya ... was that you?'

'No. But what's the difference? You had to see them sooner or later.'

You stopped trying to guess where the next few minutes might lead you. You just took a long breath, as if undertaking a labour certain to empty you of everything you have. With eyes closed, you let Cairo's air fill your lungs as you gathered the words to search for a way to describe the previous day's outing.

You'd gone to Mokattam in early evening, to give yourself the best chance of finding Ali. You clutched his letters like a talisman meant to guide you toward their author. You'd started at the house where he'd lived with his mother. Only its bare walls remained. Even the wooden window casements had been pulled off. Truly, everything got recycled here. It took only a few steps inside to see that nobody had lived there for many years. You looked around, searching for some remnant from the past: a photo still clinging to a wall, a worn-out Mohamed Mounir cassette. You found nothing. You struggled to recollect the layout of the furniture, the smell of taro simmering on the gas stove, the sound of laughter ... The cold reality of your surroundings was so unlike what you held in your memory that you began to doubt you were in the right place. You realized you were standing on the exact spot where, sixteen years earlier, the inert body of Ali's mother had lain, while you bore witness to her death, powerless to do anything for her. Your breathing was laboured now. The air seemed poisoned by an invisible evil. Death, you thought. Or worse still, the absence of life. You were struck by the feeling that your presence was desecrating a sacred place. A church that hadn't been prayed at in centuries. The temple of a god no one believed in anymore. You left immediately.

In the car we'd loaned you, you drove toward the clinic where you had once cared for the district's residents. Perhaps you were trying to remember the good works you had done on this mountain, or somehow wash away the feeling of desecration you had just experienced. Or were you maybe trying to find some person who might tell you something about Ali? Or perhaps none of these. You retraced the path he'd shown you the night you'd met, the one you'd driven hundreds of times thereafter. Along the way you saw the Islamic clinic that had been under construction when you left. It looked like it had never been finished. You parked on the right-hand side, as usual, and peered out your window. As night fell, you couldn't see inside your old clinic. Everything looked the same as it had last time you'd been there. No sooner had you placed your hand on the door handle than a deep voice rang out, spurred on by the sound of dogs barking.

'Hey, what are you looking for?'

The man's words blended in with the barking of his excited dogs. You made a gesture of appeasement as he approached. He stared at you in disbelief, then calmed his dogs with a sharp snap of his leash.

'Doctor? Is that you, doctor?'

It took you a few moments to recognize the son of old Mufid, who used to accompany his father when he came to the clinic for his arthritic fingers. When he was sure it was you, he waved the key to the room, which had kept its spot on his ring for fifteen years. Fearing that no one would believe him or, worse still, that he'd be blamed for not keeping you in the neighbourhood, he bellowed out in the powerful voice that had startled you a few minutes earlier.

'Come! Quickly! The doctor's back! What are you waiting for? You want me to pick you up one by one? Hurry up!'

Then they began arriving one by one. The first ones were curious, expecting a joke. Next came a hesitant group of ladies. One tugged on your sleeve to make you turn around. When she recognized you, she covered her flushed cheeks with her hands as if she'd witnessed an apparition. Soon dozens had gathered around you. You tried to make out their features in the dark of the night. Some were familiar, even if you had forgotten their names; others you were seeing for the first time. 'Ya doctur, are you back for good?' croaked a hoarse voice from the back. You couldn't even see the man who had just called out to you. When you could no longer produce words, you simply shook your head. Then a woman clapped her hands and started singing in Arabic that Dalida song, the one you had played in your office all those years ago, the one Sadat had played on the plane home from state visits and that the entire nation knew by heart. You hadn't heard it in years.

A few words …

A silence, and then the response, in unison.

You are beautiful, my country!

Again, silence; and then again, everyone in unison.

A few words
You are beautiful, my country!
I've always hoped
To return one day
And stay forever

You listened to the lyrics as if for the first time. You could not have sung them on your own. Your gaze fell on one woman in the crowd who you recognized right away: Amira. Your lips wrote her name as you placed your hand on your left temple, where she first felt the

migraines she had described at your consultations. Her laughter
broke out amidst the singing.

Memories of things past.
I hold on to them, my country.
My heart is full of stories.

You closed your eyes, to better concentrate on the chorus of
voices. It wasn't enough to hold back your tears.

My first love was in my country,
I'll never forget him.
What is left of the old times,
Before we parted ways?

From time to time people would confuse the lyrics, trailing off
toward the end of a line or simply clapping out the beat, encouraged
by the look or feeling on your face. You laid your hand on your
chest to show your heart was full. As if a few notes had the power
to rewrite the course of a life, they let themselves believe, for a
moment, that you might reconsider.

One or two songs –
You're beautiful, my country.

You're beautiful, my country.
Where is my sweetheart, my country?
So far from me, my country.
And whenever I sing, I think of you.

You did not look at Fatheya as you described this scene, as if
you were recounting it for your own benefit more than for hers.

You could feel the emotion stealing over you as you relived the moment.

'The few people who still remembered him said they hadn't seen him in years. And these letters … there's no address on the envelopes. How the hell is that possible, Fatheya? He's dead!'

She turned toward the church, raised her eyes to the heavens, and spoke as quietly as she could, as if she feared that, even in her coffin, her employer might catch her talking behind her back.

'Your mother saw him as a danger. She thought he'd ruin your life if your relationship went on … They came to an agreement.'

'Agreement?'

'Yes, they made an arrangement. She sent him away. And he promised not to try to see you again.'

You took a long breath. You were beginning to understand but were careful not to jump to conclusions.

'What about those letters?'

'When he learned that you'd left Cairo and there was no longer any reason for faking his death … he asked your mother if she'd let him write you. He felt guilty, wanted you to know the truth. What difference would it have made if you'd gone anyway? At first, your mother refused. But then she started to worry he'd try to find you. In the end, she took his letters when he came to Cairo. She made him believe she was passing them on to you, that you simply weren't ready to answer … '

For years she had been preparing herself for the question that would follow.

'And now, do you know where he is?'

'Yes. Well, I think so … Do you remember Dr. Darwish?'

'Papa's friend?'

'He opened a medical school near Sohag, in Upper Egypt, a few years back. Your mother sent Ali there.'

You said nothing. You felt like a foreigner in your own story, refused to let yourself be overtaken by this fresh hope. As in the parable of the kingdom of heaven, which was being recounted at that very moment by the priest in the church, you were focused on separating the wheat from the chaff. The priest fell silent. After the silence, Fatheya thought she heard my voice in the distance, reading the text I'd written for Mémie. You weren't listening. She went to add something, but stopped herself. The crowd began reciting a *Gloria Patri*, their voices mashed together, quashed by the stone walls.

Glory be to the Father,
And to the Son

You were already gone. Unbeknownst to me, you had slipped away again. I had stopped looking for you in the crowd. They were wrong, all of them were wrong: the real drama wasn't being played out around that coffin adorned with a spray of lilies, but elsewhere. Far beyond the smoke of incense.

World without end.
Amen.

38

You reached Cairo's central station as your mother was being laid to rest. You bought a ticket on the next train to Upper Egypt. It left in fifteen minutes. A boy on a stool was listening to a radio as he watched over the grandly named International Department Store, one stall of newspapers and another with small bags of food. You hadn't eaten all day. You bought a bag of chips and told the boy to keep the change. The train pulling into the station drowned out your voice. This hasty departure wasn't the first you could be accused of. What did it matter? More than enough people were gathered to celebrate death; you would rather find a way back to life.

You would have liked to go to sleep and wake up at Sohag station, but there were too many thoughts rattling around in your mind. You decided to reread Ali's letters. Only now did you understand what they were: an invitation to meet again, not bound to place or time. Now that you had at last found the place, fate would set the date. Four years had passed since his last letter. Tired of waiting for an answer, he had given up on writing to you. And just as he was renouncing any hope of a reunion, you would reappear. The thought of it made you smile like a child.

Ali. You pictured his face again. Though you had banished it from your thoughts for years, it still sometimes came back to you in the night. Perhaps you dreamed of him, just as I sometimes dreamed of you. Isn't that what dreams are for? Bringing back those who are absent? In your dreams Ali would appear out of nowhere;

you would try to take him in your arms, but that effort would wrench you from sleep. Like a candle's flame bending under a breath before vanishing, your vision was snuffed out. Tucked away in bed, you watched it burn away, at once tragic and soothing, with tears poised, waiting to fall, in the corners of your eyes.

Ali, alive ... Could you have always known, deep down, that his death had been faked? That some layer of your subconscious mind had seen through your mother's ploy? She was to blame for what had happened to you, yet you felt no bitterness. What did it profit you to hold a grudge against the dead? Your heart bore no resentment; it went on beating only to see what the coming hours held in store.

You didn't tell Dr. Darwish you were coming, not wanting to run the risk of Ali finding out. Who could say how he would react? Would he resent you for leaving his letters unanswered? Or maybe fear another of your mother's traps? You combed through his letters for a clue. You tried to imagine the ideal setting for the moment of your reunion. Would it be better to see his face in the bright light of day, or wait until evening, when the two of you might exchange confidences under cover of twilight? What if he asked you to stay with him? Would you have the courage to lay down your suitcase for good? After thinking long and hard, your answer was *yes*. You would pick up where your life had left off in the hope that your parting was like certain diseases that can be contracted only once, with lifelong immunity.

You took a few moments to bask in the sweetness of these images, before you felt an apprehension rising. An old fear, instilled in childhood, that asking too much of heaven would invite the evil eye. What if he'd left Sohag? Was there any way to be certain he hadn't moved to a new town in the last fifteen years? He could have become a doctor, bought a colleague's practice in the countryside. You reassured yourself that Dr. Darwish could surely help you find him, if needed. But what if he'd met someone since his last letter? How old was he now, thirty-six? Ali was handsome. He must have drawn admiring stares wherever he went. Your brain was a jumble of conjecture, a skein of questions leading only to further questions. Why hadn't you entertained this thought earlier? He might be married, with a family. Thirty-six ... Ali was older now than you had been when you met him. What hopes and dreams had *you* harboured at that age? What remained of that newly married doctor from Dokki who had been unable even to imagine the devastating consequences of your relationship? Next to nothing, save perhaps the same thrill you would feel at meeting the same man again. Ali, married? The image made you smile. He didn't care enough for your bourgeois comforts, wasn't the sort of bird to willingly take to a cage. But even if he had no wife and no commitments, might he not still love another? Had he found some dark-eyed man in Upper Egypt with whom to re-enact your clandestine waltzes? This final possibility shrouded your thoughts in a fog of melancholy.

You tried to see reason. If Ali told you he loved another, if he had found that affection he so deserved somewhere else, what right had you to let your disappointment taint your reunion? You'd thank fate for putting him back on your path again, and savour your good fortune to have found him alive and well. It was decided then: if Ali told you he was happy now, you wouldn't let even a hint of sadness show on your face. You would just take him in your arms for perhaps the last time, and this final time, the one life had denied you fifteen years earlier, would be precious. You'd hold him close, discreetly attempting to breathe in his scent, and you'd carefully speak to him in clear and simple words. You'd congratulate him on his wonderful news. Yes, that's how you'd phrase it: *That's great news, Ali. I wish you both a wonderful life, full of love.* As you said it, you'd smile in a way that left no doubt as to your sincerity.

Your smile might be exaggerated, unconvincing, but you'd smile all the same. From the unfathomable dark depths of your soul, you'd envy this other man's dumb luck, but you'd keep smiling all the same. And then you would leave.

❧

I asked Fatheya if you believed in God. My question terrified her, even more than when I had pronounced Ali's name in her presence.

'Of course he believes in God!' she replied, crossing herself three times as if to make it clear to the Almighty that it had all been a misunderstanding, this affront had been atoned for, and everyone in this room was a good Christian.

'Tell me, why wouldn't he believe in God?'

One absurd question begs another. The burden now fell to the prosecution.

I couldn't blame Fatheya for thinking this way; doubt has long been an enemy of religion. Why else glorify Abraham for obeying God's injunction to take his only son to Mount Moriah? Why chasten the weakness of the apostle who had to see in order to believe? My question had been innocently intended. I merely wondered whether you, too, had an invisible father, one you sometimes had conversations with.

Leaving Cairo and skipping the final tributes to your mother spared you from having to hear everyone wishing her to *rest in peace*; how could you not have felt the inanity of such wishes in her case? You knew full well she was not one for easeful rest; even after the Sunday mulukhiyah, she always slept with one eye open. What do we gain by wishing for people a state so out of character? It struck me as nonsensical to imagine some heaven where a totally different Mémie than the one I had loved might be waiting for me. And how old would she be, up there? Would she resemble the mother you had known, or the grandmother I'd just lost? If there is life after death, so much the better, but I've lived through too many hypotheses to have yet one more imposed on me.

So I can't say for sure if you believed in God on that day fifteen years earlier when your mother told you Ali was dead. Nor can I guess whether your belief was in spite of or because of his death. I can't know if you held out a hope of seeing him again, in that eternity where we're all supposed to be reunited. Or if you had prayed that he, too, might *rest in peace*.

It was more than three kilometres from Sohag's central station to the university across the Nile. A line of taxis stood waiting for the Cairo passengers, like hungry children in a dining hall at lunchtime. After agreeing on a price to take you to your hotel, you climbed into the car at the head of the line. You spent the fifteen-minute ride staring at the crowds, entertaining the possibility that Ali might be in there, somewhere. Your gaze lingered on groups of young people – as if age would not have touched the man you'd left behind. A few men gave you pause, and you were frustrated when the driver got moving again before you could chase all doubt from your mind. No matter, you wouldn't want him to see you like that, with the dark circles traced under your eyes by travel, grief, and anticipation. The taxi meter scrolled numbers to which no one paid any attention. The journey was drawing to a close. You grasped the yellowing bills, slightly more than the agreed-upon amount.

You placed your suitcase at the foot of the bed but didn't bother unpacking. You gazed out at the view from your bedroom. Two fishermen in a shaky boat were casting their net, gliding along on the Nile's gentle swell under a cloudless sky. You opened the French window and stepped out onto the balcony. Leaning against the wrought-iron railing, you looked down on the people walking along the river. Here, two lovers strolling by; there, a woman staring out at the river, embroidering. You sat with your thoughts for a few moments, then went back into the room. The telephone was on a large console table. You stared at it, longing for the news it might bring you. You had a plan to call the university registrar's office to get Ali's address, in case Dr. Darwish wasn't there to see you. That proved unnecessary; he answered after a few rings. He offered you an appointment in a few hours, didn't ask your reasons. Your name alone – or your father's, strictly speaking – was enough. Or maybe the doctor had an inkling of why you were there.

39

Montreal, 2000

The acoustic tiles of the suspended ceiling echo the patterns on the gleaming floor. It is all so familiar that Viviane Daniels barely notices. She moves through the corridors of the Royal Vic hospital, pushing her cart and occasionally swearing. Though English is her first language, she is equally free with the Québécois curse words, happy to make sure no one is left out.

Viviane replaces a small notice that has slipped out of its metal frame. To ensure patient confidentiality, please wait here. *Here is a line of tape on the floor. It has bunched up in places. Viviane's cart often catches on this here. A letter for Dr. Seidah arrived three days earlier, but he was on vacation. An Egyptian stamp. Viviane did not place it into the doctor's pigeonhole, per the usual procedure. If you'd asked her why, she wouldn't have known what to say. But no one asks. On her way upstairs, she sees a light on in his office. He seems to be immersed in a pre-op report.*

'*Aren't you on vacation?*'

'*I cut it short.*'

'*Sounds like you! You finally take a vacation and then ... You could have used the rest!*'

'*I don't see the patients taking vacations ...* '

'*That's why they need their doc to be rested.*'

'*You've got an answer for everything.*'

'*Yup. I've even got some mail for you!*'

She removes several envelopes from her metal divider and hands them to him.

'Thanks, Viviane.'

He places the envelopes on his desk and turns back to his screen.

'Did you see this one? You have some external mail, too.'

'You're such a busybody!'

'Well, well … I guess I'd better finish my rounds! Have a nice day, doc.'

'Have a good one.'

He speaks in a neutral tone, without looking up from his screen. He waits a few minutes for her to move along, then takes out the pale yellow envelope whose Egyptian stamp has clearly piqued his co-worker's curiosity.

Cairo, August 9, 2000

Dear Dr. Seidah,

I have received your letter and understand that your time is precious. I don't intend to take up too much of it, but it would mean a lot to me if you would reconsider your position. I don't believe I mentioned it, but my report is focused on doctors treating patients with Huntington's disease. I understand that this cause is close to your heart.

I look forward to your response, and hope it will be affirmative.

Sincerely,
Ahmed Naguib

40

Writing is nothing but a pain. That's not my theory, it's Fatheya's. At first, I thought I could find a way to tell your story. Choose all the right words, noble phrases like the ones in the French tragedies that line Mémie's oak bookshelves. And I thought that would be enough. I could write down what I knew about you, invent the rest, make excuses, describe you as I might have liked you to be. I was even more naive to believe I could stay outside the story's frame. Ridiculous! There's no way to stay outside your own story. Everything that came before – the things that you missed, the things that formed you. What comes out in the telling *is* the author's own story. You strip away the trappings of convention, keep the parts that ring true. Whatever isn't plausible, or doesn't explain what is or could have been, serves no purpose. We tear up entire pages whose cleverness is contrived, pages of copping out and shying away from the truth, only to realize at the end that we have described the contours of our own hatreds as much as the cowardice of others. And at the end of the process, our one reward is exhaustion.

'Why are you writing all this? Are you sure it's healthy to be stirring up these old stories?'

'No, I'm not sure … '

'And it's not like it'll bring him back, right?'

'Yeah, I know.'

'Well, it looks like nothing but a pain to me. But that's your business!'

For weeks, I stopped writing. I needed to understand why I was telling you into existence, why I was trying so hard to decipher the past at an age when all my friends were looking toward their futures. Then I came back to Fatheya, thinking I'd found the answer to her question. I told her that we all deserve to see the world in our own light. Your light had too often been blocked out by human folly, or scheming, or implacable fate. It was important for me to give you back a touch of the light that the world did not want to see.

Though she usually laughed at my grandiloquent phrases, Fatheya fell silent. I think she could see what I meant. Yet as I write these next few lines, I can sense that my flame will once again blow out before having the chance to produce any real heat or light. So I'll be brief.

As you might have expected, your premature departure from the funeral caused a stir. Only Fatheya knew the reason, and since no one would have thought to ask her, she didn't even have to lie. I was the only one she told about your conversation, right when we got home. In other words, the news that Ali's death had been staged was revealed to you and to me just hours apart. Fatheya was telling me the last secret she knew about you, a secret that outlived Mémie by a matter of days. I might have expected this confession to come as a relief, but her face suddenly resembled that of an old woman, as if she hadn't shed so much a weight as a vital part of her life. She handed me a piece of paper with the phone number she'd given you earlier, stood up with some difficulty, collected her things from the hallway, and went home. She didn't even try to gauge the effect of her revelations. She'd done what she had to. The rest was up to me.

Since it was late, I waited until the next day to call Dr. Darwish. He had only just met you, but he repeated what he'd told you. He told me about Ali, how your mother had asked him to look after him, how he'd accepted out of friendship with your late father. All Mémie had told him was that Ali was interested in medicine, knew some basics, and would be delighted to assist the doctor in his practice, if he saw the opportunity. And so it went. For a boy with no formal instruction, Ali had shown impressive dexterity. He was clearly repeating procedures he had learned elsewhere, though he was always cagey about the circumstances.

A new medical school was slated to open in Sohag in 1992. Dr. Darwish was personally invested in this massive project, which would take years to complete. So, in addition to assisting the doctor in his practice, Ali ended up helping him at the new medical school: administrative tasks, some secretarial work, and other errands. One thing that never ceased to amaze Dr. Darwish was how thoroughly this boy from a poor background, who had learned to read only late in life, had mastered the mores of the upper middle classes. One day, he had the idea of putting together an application for his assistant to join the faculty's first class of students. He supported an equivalency application that would take into account the years of working under him, and even secured a scholarship. While Ali would never have put it in quite those terms, it was clearly a dream come true.

From time to time Dr. Darwish broke off in his account, as if he feared losing the thread. For the first two years, Ali had excelled, outstripping even the sons of good families who had attended top schools in Cairo or Alexandria. But then he began showing symptoms. Motor difficulties at first, then cognitive problems that worried the doctor more. Though the onset was uncharacteristically early, it looked like Huntington's disease. This diagnosis was supported by the probable family history. It soon became clear Ali could never practise medicine. Ali hadn't needed to be told; he'd seen the disease's progress with his mother and knew what to expect. The doctor tried to find other work for him to do, but it was difficult to broach the subject with Ali. He was too proud; he was allergic to pity.

In early 1997, Ali was found in the Nile, drowned. It was impossible to say whether it was a desperate choice or a stupid accident, as his motor problems had taken a sharp turn for the worse the previous year. I was given to understand that the doctor believed the former. Without knowing the exact nature of my relationship to Ali, he handled his words with surgical care.

'You mustn't judge him. Everyone deals with illness in their own way, and Ali showed great courage. He was a good boy, very diligent … I'm glad to see that there are people who care about him today. I didn't know he had any family or friends. We gave him a proper burial. I got the faculty to cover part of the cost; your grandmother, God rest her soul, contributed as well. I think he used to visit her when he was in Cairo: he once sent me her greetings. By the way, I heard from Tarek that you were in mourning. I do hate to add this bad news, on top of that … '

Dr. Darwish had to go, but he invited me to call back that evening if I had further questions. What other questions could I possibly have? I thanked him and hung up. I remembered Ali's letters, the allusions to his mother that I hadn't understood. I saw once more the urgency in your eyes, when you had left Mémie's apartment after finding them. I imagined the emptiness you felt when you heard the news, just moments before I did. You'd left Cairo to find the one you loved most in the world; he had just died a second time.

41

Our memories have no worth save for those who live on in them. Once those people are gone, memories of them become currency, a play money not to be mistaken for the real thing. When Ali disappeared fifteen years earlier, you decided to bury your time together in a remote corner of your mind: somewhere off the map, some secret location where no one could ever dig it up. Yet in mere hours, Ali had come back from the dead. He'd turned you into a crazed old man, desperate to recover the treasure he'd thrown away, thinking it was worthless. For as long as this illusion persisted, you had been digging with bare hands in the siliceous soil of your memory. You dug until your fingers were bloody and your mind in agony. My heart sinks at the thought of you getting ready to experience the resurrection of a man who was, in fact, gone for good.

Now that the mirage had dissipated, you almost doubted that Ali had ever lived. You took his letters from their envelopes one last time. They were the sole material manifestation of your love, the fragile thread you might in another time have pulled, forcing life to lead you back to each other once more. Had he understood, in the end, that his letters had never been passed on to you? He must have at least entertained the thought. He certainly knew his words would be read by your mother: the fear of censorship pervaded every word. When he wrote, 'I thought of you the other day,' it meant *I have not forgotten you; I cannot forget you. Just tell me you don't blame me.* Even the most innocuous turns of phrase had been stripped of all illusion.

In a last-ditch effort, you tried to understand what could have led up to this faked death fifteen years earlier. Your mind struggled to recreate the conversation that had sealed your history, the cruel bargain Ali must have struck with your mother. You were now as powerless as I am, forced to reconstruct the scenes that had shaped your destiny without your being there to experience them.

You imagined your mother making her way to Mokattam. In that foreign land, she would have pushed open the door of a house where you had so often eaten, not waiting for an invitation to hang her fur coat on a chair. With what words had she convinced him to disappear? Had she resorted to threats, or to bribes? It wasn't like Ali to submit to orders. So what could she have said? Had she suggested that earning a degree would be his one chance of becoming a doctor? It was possible. Had she told him that he was jeopardizing your relationship, your reputation, your family? Undoubtedly. That, if he truly loved you, it was the only thing to do? Is there a world in which she would have described the bond you shared with the verb *love*?

He could have simply put an end to your relationship, made some excuse, and disappeared. But he must have suspected you would never let him go. That, even if he managed to disappear, you would do whatever it took to track him down. Your mother must have come to a similar conclusion, for there was no doubt that this *mise en scène* bore her signature. The fake death, the real departure, the hope that her son would come to his senses … Ever meticulous, she must have thought through every detail of her plan before convincing Ali to take part. The situation had become untenable for you both. This faked death was the only way out. Ali had simply accepted a helping hand.

The more you thought it over, the less you were inclined to blame Ali. After all, what reason did he have to refuse? The job you were offering him? Your clandestine nights of love that held out no hope of a future? The imbalance of your lives had made you feel like Ali's benefactor, but what had you ever really done for him, when you got down to it? To the doctor, he was a mere assistant. To the man, a lover. You had confined him to making do with the crumbs of your life, to be forever stuck in unambitious supporting roles. You'd never given up anything for him. You'd only ever shared a little of your stifling present; your mother was offering a future. You came to wonder whether, in the end, she hadn't been more generous than you.

42

Montreal, 2000

من أنت؟

In Arabic, two words sufficed to ask, Who are you? *Tarek slips them into an envelope to drop off at the post office at the end of his workday. There's one on the ground floor of the building where the Huntington Society of Quebec has its office. He has to go that very evening, to give a training session for caregivers and health-care professionals. That leaves time to go home and change.*

With its usual mechanical hiccup, his building's elevator opens onto the fifth floor. Tarek gets out, turns left, opens the second door, and places his belongings on the dining room table. The walls are white: no picture frames, no coloured paint, no photographs or plants, just a few medical books in an IKEA *bookcase. A window offers glimpses of fall colours in the treetops. He flips on the radio. They're talking about the death of Pierre Elliott Trudeau. He turns it off and puts on a tape he'd found the day before. The first notes transport him to the past. He rewinds and starts the song from the beginning. It's Dalida singing her love of a country he, too, has known. He sinks into the steam of a shower that he knows will be brief.*

43

No one ever really makes peace with grief; we simply come to terms with our mortality. At times we may even find something approaching serenity. Now and then we cry. We cry to feel alive, to remind ourselves that we have been spared, for now, and to measure how narrowly we have escaped. We say that we cry for the ones who have left us. But the truth is that we only ever weep for our own powerlessness.

Infants know instinctively that crying is the shortest path to sleep. It's a resounding cry from the depths of the psyche, one that no diversion will calm. A cry eager to attain the state of exhaustion it is sure to bring about, and impervious to consolation since the crier is in no way sad. A cry that pays no heed to this absurd misinterpretation. A cry of selfishness.

You must have cried when you heard the news, but in all truth I can feel myself losing my ability to conceive of your life from that point on. Up till then, I had been able to imagine it by piecing together, as best I could, what little I had: Fatheya's contradictory accounts, my handful of photos of you, Ali's letters, and the innuendo, like a chemical solution in which my own childhood had been soaked. I had created for myself the father life denied me, leading a parallel existence to which I was barred access. At first, I did it for myself, convinced that this equation with a thousand unknowns could yield only one answer, the inspiring presence my life had lacked up to here. Later, without realizing it, I began to do it for you. Like sticking up for a father subjected to insults in the classroom; like rehabilitating the reputation of a man no longer there to defend himself; like unconditionally supporting a loved one. Yet what did you and I have in common? You weren't close to me, quite the opposite: a faraway presence. You were a distant person I somehow, inexplicably, cared about. The sum of my inferences had ended up revealing a story: yours. Or, more precisely, *my* story of you. It had been transformed into a truth at once splendid and fragile, a towering statue with feet of iron and clay the likes of which I'd never thought possible outside the gilt-edged pages of my grandmother's missal.

But all that had now come to an end. It now seemed as if the weight of the slightest additional assumption might shatter this unstable likeness. So I stopped inventing. I was unable to put myself in your shoes, to decide whether you'd gone to lay flowers on Ali's second grave, to imagine the tenor of your mental state, the rage or despair that gripped you in the end. Did you contemplate joining him in the Nile, which had taken him away from you for a second time? Or had his death shown you with a new and violent clarity that, for you, there would be no escaping life? Did you try to reconstruct his life in Sohag? Or just rush back to Montreal to save what was left of your own?

I'm going to stop writing about your life now, because there are things words cannot do. Words can't bring back from the dead the ones who have left us. They can't heal the sick or redress injustice, just as it is absurd to claim the dead can either start wars or end them. In any case, words are at best a symptom and at worst a pretext. I am going to stop writing your life because it isn't mine to tell, because it's the sum of an improbable blend of your bad luck and bad decisions, because even the most abject among us would never wish to take your place. Because you can't fill an absence with sentences. I'm going to stop writing your life because it's been undermined by too many lies for me to add more of my own, even with the best of intentions. I'm going to stop writing your life because I need you to tell me your story, because I no longer want any version but your own. If you are reading me, it means that I've succeeded, that we've sat down together, that I've freed myself from the reams of paper accumulated over so many years, that I've finally found a way to tell you who I am, that I've pushed you to find in me a resemblance to you and to my mother.

I tremble at the thought of succeeding; I shudder at the thought that these words will never be read. I've missed you, Father.

44

Montreal, 2001

A chintzy Christmas tree's synthetic boughs strain under the weight of its dollar-store balls. Caregivers and patients walk around it, paying no heed. The new year is just a few weeks old, but time is measured differently in hospitals. Those who know they're getting out one day try to kill it; others fight to gain even the smallest of portions. They inject it in their veins, tweak it from blood test to blood test, come to terms with it, and sometimes let it slip between their fingers.

A courier hurries toward the front desk. On the window, there are streaks of faux-snow patterns and a message inviting him to press the bell for assistance if no agent is present. No agent is present. The courier presses the button. A few words escape the small speaker in the Plexiglas barrier: 'Hello, how can I help you?' A woman's voice, an indifferent tone. He needs a signature; she exits the desk area through a side door. Dr. Seidah is in surgery. Viviane will wait until the end of the day to take him the parcel.

45

Cairo, 2001

'What are you doing?'

She was standing in the doorway. My first instinct was to turn over the notepad I'd been writing in, to let her know she'd frightened me. In our new apartment, where we lived on a single floor, there was a guest room next to mine. Nesrine stayed there sometimes, when the evening meal went late and she didn't want to make her driver wait.

She was standing there calmly with her hand still on the door-knob. Her silence seemed to imply that I hadn't answered her. I made something up.

'I'm finishing my homework … '

'On stationery?' She smiled. 'It's not a love letter that's keeping you awake at night, is it?'

I didn't answer.

'You're writing to Tarek.'

It wasn't a question, nor a reproach. Her voice had a confident gentleness. I was astonished, almost less by her knowing what I was doing than the fact that she pronounced your first name. I think it was the first time that it had happened in my presence. You were no longer *he*, no longer *my brother*, no longer an unspoken presence beneath the surface of my family's words that I pretended not to understand. To Nesrine, your sister, who now knew I was writing to you, you were *Tarek*. I felt almost relieved. Without actually pushing my hand, she moved it along with hers, encouraging it to turn over the pad of paper. I opened my palm, inviting her to take it. Her eyebrows furrowed after reading the first few words. She reread them in silence.

46

She is in the doorway, waving a cardboard brick stamped with Arabic characters. He invites her in. It may not be a pale yellow envelope this time, but he has no doubt the sender is the same.

'What is it?'

She answers with a curt wave that could mean How should I know? *Or maybe* Just keep it up and I'll open the damn box myself! *He pretends not to notice her curiosity, shakes the parcel next to his right ear, and shrugs his shoulders, as if he will never again speak another word. He is toying with her impatience. Finally, he opens the box.*

'A watch?'

It's not just any watch, though. Now it's his turn to not answer. His brow furrows as he turns the pocket watch over to check for the initials he knows he will find there. His father's, before they were his own. Only the tinkling sound of the watch chain troubles their silence. Viviane breaks it, at last.

'The journalist again?'

'If he's a journalist, I'm a prima ballerina ... '

'What's going on?'

He seems to be following a train of thought, but lets it drop.

'Someone who likes to play games, clearly ... or wants to go back in time.'

With his thumbnail, he absent-mindedly opens and then closes the watch clasp.

'Are you worried about it?'

'No. Honestly, few things worry me. Pocket watches aren't one of them.'

A semblance of a smile flits across his face. Viviane isn't always receptive to his humour. He grows serious again.

'If he really wanted to worry me, he'd go about it differently. Or that's my guess, at least.'

'Okay, I'm glad. I wouldn't have wanted you to … Well, at least it's a nice watch!'

She pretends to be reassured and finishes her break. She has already gone over her time. He waits to hear the elevator doors close before opening his desk drawer. He takes out the photo that came with the second letter. He stares at it for a very long time, as if trying to locate some specific detail, some answer. Perhaps confirmation.

The box with the watch also holds two sheets of paper, which he was careful not to take out in front of Viviane. He unfolds the first, recognizing the black-and-white brochure for the American medical conference on Huntington's disease that he's scheduled to attend in Boston in September. The event dates are highlighted, as is his name among the speakers. The second sheet is smaller in size, a handwritten note on stationery.

'I'd love to meet you there. Would you be available for coffee on Tuesday morning, at eight-thirty?'

The address of an Irish pub is written at the bottom of the message, the only Latin letters on the page.

47

Cairo, 2001

There was so much for me to tell, leading up to the letter I'd been writing when Nesrine walked in on me. I proceeded in chronological order. In the beginning was your absence, and my need to get to know you. Then Fatheya's confidences, Ali's letters – so many scraps of your existence. Piecing them together had become necessary. There was no judgment in my aunt's eyes, just a kindness that gave me the courage to go on telling my story. Sometimes her gaze clouded over, as she felt the accumulated weight of the unspoken words of my childhood. I didn't try to figure out what had brought her to my room at that exact moment. Maybe she'd already figured out part of what I was about to tell her. It didn't really matter.

Talking about you raised a thousand questions, as writing your life had exposed a thousand gaps I'd sidestepped with a thousand guesses. But it was too soon to ask Nesrine to shed light on the grey areas. Too soon to pit the father of my imagination against his sister's calcified memories. Nesrine listened to me without interrupting. I kept on going, trying to contain the emotion that swept over me as my story caught up with the present day. There was the meeting I had set up in Cairo, a failure despite my high hopes. Your departure for Sohag. Dr. Darwish's revelations ...

Nesrine remained silent a few moments, as if my insoluble problem was becoming her own. Finally, she pointed to the letter I was writing, the one where I'd asked you to meet me.

'What's this, then?'

I blushed before revealing the final act of my scheme.

'I made him believe I was a journalist, writing an article on Egyptian doctors … It was the best way I could come up with to make contact with him. He wrote back. There's a conference in Boston in the fall. I'm going to ask him out for a coffee. If he doesn't answer, I'll go see his talk and then go up to him afterwards. I know Maman would never let me go to Montreal: she'd see right through it. But Boston … Besides, it's right before school starts again. A chance like this won't come around again any time soon. I can't wait any longer, you know? I need to see him, talk to him … '

Our conversation trickled along without ever quite fully drying up. I could feel my aunt's confusion. All at once she had discovered both the quest that had secretly occupied my adolescence and the dizzying turn it was soon to take. True to habit, she curled a lock of hair around her index finger, trying to tease out the meaning of my last words. My determination was total, dissuasion was futile; sabotaging my departure would only postpone it. Sooner or later, this grenade was going to blow. All that was left was to direct it to where it would do the least damage.

'And how do you plan to get there? Where will you stay? What will you do for money, and everything? What will you tell your mother?'

I preferred not to go into the details of my plans. I didn't want to frighten her any further and, with just a few weeks to go, there was still a lot left to figure out. I shrugged.

'All I know is that I miss him … I mean, he's something missing in my life.'

'You've only got one life to live, Rafik. All that matters is to make one that's true to yourself … '

Nesrine was looking at me, as if searching my face for some trace of the past. In recent years, people had stopped saying how much I looked like my mother. Adolescence was blurring the features I shared with a woman oblivious to her son's torment. Now Nesrine would have to choose a side. Would she stay loyal to me or to Mira? Love and exasperation were battling for control of her smile. At last she spoke.

'Look, I'll pay for your trip to Boston. I'll talk your mother into it, it'll be your seventeenth-birthday present … But not a word of this, understand? You chose the destination. I had nothing to do with it.'

Before she could even finish, I'd already wrapped my arms around my aunt. I just wanted to thank her, but I felt my tears welling up and no way to stop them. As if only when my muscles relaxed after all these years did they become aware of the powerful tension that had always been there, pulling on them. I was crying the way you do at sixteen, when you have only just unlearned how to cry. Nesrine tenderly ran her hand down my back as she finished what she had to say.

'Just take care of yourself, that's all. And write to me and your mother every day! And don't do anything stupid! You can't control how *he* will react … '

I wondered how you'd react if I couldn't control my tears when I met you. Is a son allowed to cry in front of his father?

US

48

Cairo, 2001

A plane taxis down the runway, weaving nonchalantly between the flashing lights of vehicles driven by men in fluorescent vests. Just about everything else is grey: the asphalt scarred with dirty white smears, the control tower, the metal stairs leading to the runway … The only splash of colour is the logo of the bank on the jet bridges. Has anyone ever chosen their bank based on the ads in airport hallways?

Economy class, nine seats per row. A young man sits staring out of a window on the right-hand side. He's just gone through the usual checks, metal detectors that failed to ring. Seeing his pensive expression, the pilot had offered him a tour of the cockpit. He'd declined, with an intimidated smile, and gone to his seat. It's the start of a month, the end of an afternoon. The sun washes over half his face. In the pre-recorded welcome message, the British-accented female voice elegantly elides the *r* in *passenger*. The orange sunset storms the plane, slipping through any available opening. Next, a staticky message in a female voice with an Egyptian accent delivers the flight instructions; when she speaks, the *p* in *passengers* becomes a *b*. The sun keeps pushing forward. The voice doesn't stop. The young man doesn't listen. On this September day, he doesn't know what shape the world will take, but he can sense that it will never be the same again.

The aircraft continues along slowly, then accelerates over several hundred metres and takes off. The voice has asked for the seats to be returned to the upright position for takeoff. Despite his best efforts, the young man's seat won't budge. A broken handle. EgyptAir. When he gets off the plane a few hours later, he'll absent-mindedly answer the flight attendant who wishes him a pleasant stay. It will be the last time he speaks Arabic. For now, he's just trying to fall asleep.

49

I must have been five or six. I couldn't say what sent me running into her room, but I remember catching my mother crying. The familiar smell of bleach from the ensuite bathroom. Just like every time she tried to camouflage the sound of her suffering, her television was on, full blast. A voice engorged with patriotic fervour was sententiously reading the news. Egypt was making peace with everyone. Algeria, Syria, Libya … It would help Israel make peace with Palestine. All would be forgiven. That was something to celebrate. I didn't care. My task was far more important.

She didn't give me answers to questions I wouldn't have known how to phrase anyway. Mira, Mira, little star, how I wonder what you are. She smiled at me, making no attempt to hide her tears. I clowned around a little, typical antics of a five- or six-year-old trying to distract his mother from her sorrow. It made her laugh. Mission accomplished. In a sense, it was our first chance at a reunion. You were the tear, I the laughter. And on my mother's face, we almost met.

Now here we are again, *almost* on the verge of meeting once more. I imagined a thousand ways I might approach you, and behind each of them I heard Fatheya's old joke. *Hey, Goha! Where's your ear?* So I'd keep it simple. I'd address you in Mémie's French. I'd tell you my name, that I'm your son, and that we've got some catching up to do.

I'm sitting in this Irish pub, scribbling on a blank sheet of paper to calm my anxiety. In front of me I've placed my cardboard portfolio, grown fat with the pages on which I've gathered what I know about you. However this story ends, these will be the last words I write you. The thought that you might not come is nagging at me. I can't tell if your failure to appear would bring me devastation or relief. It might be better if I never met you – like that trip to Paris, which could only be more magical in Mémie's imaginings than it could ever have been if we'd actually taken it. Go figure.

I had ordered a coffee. The waiter began asking me questions in English. I couldn't tell if he wanted to start a conversation or just clarify the order. My heart was pounding, I felt like I was about to start an exam but didn't know the subject. I just repeated myself, 'Coffee,' with a hand movement imploring him not to ask any more questions.

'Just coffee.'

He smiled, showed me with a gesture that he would bring it over to the table of my choice. I found one facing the door, so I wouldn't miss your arrival, but far enough back to talk to you discreetly. Talk to you. You.

Now it's twelve minutes past eight. You'll either be here soon or never come.

50

Boston, 2001

A man pushes open the door. At fifty-two, the leanness that has long given him an athletic figure now accentuates every expression on his face. His eyes methodically scan the pub. His gaze settles on a table occupied by a young man who does not know, at that moment, whether to stand up or sit. Or wave. Or say something. Or claim it was all a big misunderstanding, pay for his coffee, and disappear ... Everything is serious, at seventeen. None of this will be necessary. He looks less confident here than in the photo in the man's pocket. The man understands. He walks over. He smiles. A gentle smile. Holds out his hand.

'You must be Rafik? Sorry, I'm a little late.'

Past, present, future: time is a human grammar, a universal fiction; a false proof, a true religion. But in what time scale does this moment belong? He places a pocket watch on the table. He has had his son's initials inscribed, below his father's. Soon they will be talking. Perhaps each one will let out phrases long saved up, along with others that come to them spontaneously. For the ones that slip their minds, they promise each other there will be future opportunities. They'll probably hug each other, too, moved by the unreal evidence of this moment. Mektoub, *it is written.* Deep down, each of them will hear this word pronounced in the voice of a woman who was a mother to one, a grandmother to the other.

But for now, with his incredulous gaze, the teenager seems to be asking a question. A question that begins with a *Who* … 'Who told you?'

From this point on, he will know to be wary of simple questions.

AUTHOR'S ACKNOWLEDGEMENTS

I would like to thank everyone who supported me in this writing project. Their encouragement and expressions of affection have sustained me.

I am especially grateful to Catherine, Gilbert, Mona, and Julien, whose patient, passionate, and profound engagement with my story has helped shape it over the years.

TRANSLATOR'S ACKNOWLEDGEMENTS

Thanks to the book's editor, Alana Wilcox, for her close reading and patient attention. Thanks also to everyone at Coach House, including Crystal Sikma, James Lindsay, and Stuart Ross.

I am grateful to Mary Thaler, Bronwyn Haslam, and Aleshia Jensen, who read and gave suggestions on sections of an early draft, and to Catherine Leroux for advice at a critical juncture.

On the transliteration of Arabic words and names, I would like to thank Mina Athanassious for his observations and recommendations. Transliteration is a balancing act between best practices and entrenched usage; all responsibility for choices or errors of transliteration is my own.

Finally, my heartfelt thanks to the author for his generous help throughout the process.

Born in Montreal to Egyptian parents, **Éric Chacour** has shared his life between France and Quebec. A graduate in applied economics and international relations, he now works in the financial sector. *What I Know About You* is his first novel.

Pablo Strauss's recent translations of fiction from Quebec include *The Second Substance, Aquariums, Fauna,* and *The Dishwasher.* He is a three-time finalist for the Governor General's Literary Award for translation. Pablo grew up in Victoria, BC, and has lived in Quebec City for two decades.

Typeset in Arno and Aboreto.

Printed at the Coach House on bpNichol Lane in Toronto, Ontario, on FSC-certified Sustana recycled paper, which was manufactured in Saint-Jérôme, Quebec. This book was printed with vegetable-based ink on a 1973 Heidelberg KORD offset litho press. Its pages were folded on a Baumfolder, gathered by hand, bound on a Sulby Auto-Minabinda, and trimmed on a Polar single-knife cutter.

Coach House is located in Toronto, which is on the traditional territory of many nations, including the Mississaugas of the Credit, the Anishnabeg, the Chippewa, the Haudenosaunee, and the Wendat peoples, and is now home to many diverse First Nations, Inuit, and Métis peoples. We acknowledge that Toronto is covered by Treaty 13 with the Mississaugas of the Credit. We are grateful to live and work on this land.

Translated by Pablo Strauss
Edited by Alana Wilcox
Cover design by David Drummond, cover images from Shutterstock
Interior design by Crystal Sikma
Author photo by Justine Latour
Translator photo by Charles-Frédérick Ouellet

Coach House Books
80 bpNichol Lane
Toronto ON M5S 3J4
Canada

mail@chbooks.com
www.chbooks.com